Until the Next Time 2: God's Plan

Also by Assuanta Collins

Until the Next Time

Until the Next Time 2: God's Plan
Assuanta Collins

ASTA PUBLICATIONS

Published by Asta Publications, LLC
P.O. Box 1735
Stockbridge, Georgia
www.astapublications.com

Publisher's note

This is a work of fiction. All events and characteristics in this story are solely the product of the author's imagination. Any similarities between any characters and situations presented in this book to any individuals, living or dead, or actual places and situations are purely coincidental.

Edited by Carla Dean
Cover design: Crystal Iglar
Text and composition: Kim Nakiya Howard-Carswell

Library of Congress Cataloging in Publication Data
Collins, Assuanta
    Until The Next Time 2: God's Plan: a novel / Assuanta Collins
    p. cm.
ISBN: 13 978-0-9777060-3-7
ISBN: 0-9777060-3-6
LCCN: 2007903786

First Asta Publications, LLC trade paperback edition July 2007
1. African American women-Fiction. 2. African American families-Fiction. 3. Self-realization-Fiction. 4.Drama-Ficition. 5. Urban-Fiction. 6. International-Fiction. 7. New York-Fiction. I. Title

This book is dedicated to:

Most importantly GOD for giving me the gift to tell another story.

My parents Douglas and Thelma Howard for their encouragement and support.

My husband Clayton Collins for allowing me to step out on faith.

My daughters Michaelle and Taylor for being my inspiration.

My sister Kim Nakiya Howard-Carswell for all of her support and maintaining my public image.

My brother Douglas II ....Keep your head up.

Until the Next Time 2: God's Plan

Prologue

November 17, 2002

Dearest Sonia,

I am so sorry about all of this. I never wanted our lives to turn out this way. Remember when we used to smoke Newport's and drink cherry Kool-Aid? You told me you wanted to be a doctor, and I wanted to be a pilot. The reason I wanted to be a pilot is because I wanted to fly away from all of the pain I was feeling at the time. You told me that I could be anything I wanted to be, and I believed you. When I ran away from home the day my mother came back from jail, you just held me in your arms. Those are the days I want to remember. I think you realized at the time how much you really meant to me. We were inseparable back then, and you even let me hide in your closet for one week until Ashley threatened to tell on us. Remember?

I am sorry about Ashley. I tried to stop Sharon. I never wanted anyone to get hurt. Ashley was like my little sister, and I am so sorry, Sonia. I didn't mean it. I've never been in jail before, and I am so scared, baby. I wish you were here to hold me and tell me everything is going to be okay.

Sonia, you grew up, and I was afraid you were going to leave me. I wanted my little girlfriend back, the one who was so innocent and believed I could become a pilot. You were so sweet, and you wouldn't sleep with me for six months. I respected you and knew at that moment you would become my wife. Sonia, I wish I could turn back the hands of time, but I can't, so I am saying wouldn't sleep with me for six months. I respected you and knew at that moment you would become my wife. Sonia, I wish I could turn back the hands of time, but I can't, so I am saying goodbye. Please tell Jasmine that Daddy loves her and he is sorry for leaving her this way. I can no longer live with this pain, and it will be better for us all if I kill myself. Last thing, tell the police that Maritza killed Red and you can find her in the basement of our old apartment building in The Bronx.

I will always love you, Sonia.

Your Loving Husband,
Mark

I don't know why I continue to read Mark's farewell letter. Every time I read it, I cry. I know there was nothing I could have done to help him. Mark provided me with the closure I needed.

Today is August 1, 2005, and it's Ashley's birthday. She would have been thirty-three years old if my husband's girlfriend did not kill her. I still recall the last conversation we had.

"Ashley, how are you doing? Have you received any strange calls lately?" I inquired.

"I'm fine. How did you know about the phone call? Some chick named Sharon called and said if you did not divorce Mark, she would kill you. I didn't take her seriously. I told her to quit fucking around and to grow the fuck up. She called me a fucking dyke and hung the phone up. Who the fuck did she think she was threatening?"

"Ashley, Sharon is a crazy bitch. She had some thugs fuck Desmond up. She is serious about doing bodily harm to anyone that gets in her way. I am going to give him the divorce. He has been nothing but trouble and I don't need his ass anymore. We need to get the fuck out of here. Tracy suggested that we take a trip someplace until the dust settles."

Ashley never made it to my house. As Ashley attempted to leave the apartment, Sharon and Mark attacked her. When Tracy, my best friend arrived at Ashley's apartment Sharon and Mark ran out and Ashley was on the floor in a pool of blood. According to Tracy, my best friend, Sharon sliced Ashley's throat with a meat cleaver.

Chapter 1

Samantha, Ashley's girlfriend, calls me every year to reminisce and cry over how much we miss her and what we would do to get her back. Samantha and Ashley were only together for two months when she died, and she has been holding a torch all this time. Ashley's death caused emotional distress for Samantha, to the point she moved into Ashley's apartment. My mother said she thought Samantha was a lunatic because she kept everything the same as it was before Ashley died. Mom was upset by it and threatened to take Samantha to court, but I convinced her to leave it alone. Samantha agreed to allow my mother to take a few of Ashley's belongings, but Mom wanted Samantha to move out of the apartment and turn over all of Ashley's belongings to her. Everyone handles death differently, and I understood my mother for wanting Ashley's precious items. It has been difficult for me, too, and I have not gone back to New York because the memories are painful.

"Good morning, Sonia. I've been thinking about you a lot lately. How are you and Ajani doing? I can't believe you are still living in England. When are you guys going to tie the knot? Don't you miss the good ol' United States?"

"Good morning, Samantha. Ajani hasn't proposed to me yet, and I think I am going to leave him this time. His regiment of having different women and late night meetings are taking a toll on me. Mark taught me well, and I refuse to marry another cheating man. I miss my mother, and it would have been nice if she stayed in England with us. Life in the UK agrees with my peace of mind. I had the usual nightmare last night, and I wonder if it will ever stop."

"I doubt you will ever stop having those nightmares. You will mourn Ashley for the rest of your life, Sonia, and you need to see a professional to help you cope. Therapy will help you deal with the lost, and you will learn to stop blaming yourself. I surely miss her, too, and have been seeing a professional for three years, which has helped. I miss the times when we would cuddle each other after playing a good ol' game of Othello, but I know she is no longer with me, so I have to move on. We were only together for a short time, but I knew she was my soul mate. It is a shame that we will never have the opportunity to grow old together. My therapist helped me to recognize the time we spent together and to stop blaming myself for her death. I often thought if I were here, she would be alive today.

"Ashley and I didn't play hooky from work often, but since we were both working so many hours, we decided we needed some "us time". We went to the Metropolitan Art Museum and marveled over Pablo Picasso's Night Fishing at Antibes (1939), Piet Mondrian's Broadway Boogie Woogie (1942–43), and Roy Lichtenstein's Interior with Mobile (1992). Our day at the museum left us famished, so we went to Awash, our favorite Ethiopian restaurant. Normally, we make reservations because the place is usually standing room only with college students, but we were fortunate to get a table rather quickly. What I love about the place is the ambience and the modern décor. The country-like setting would make the most unromantic person romantic. Portraits of past Emperors adorn the wall, giving you a sense of security as you eat your food. Ashley wanted your mother to respect our relationship and hurt each time she questioned our love. Let me tell you this, your sister and I loved each other, and she was not ashamed to show affection in public or in your mother's presence. Your mother upsets me with her backward thinking and judgmental ways, and I am so glad I don't have to deal with her anymore."

"Yeah, well, my mother has a way of getting underneath people's skin. She grew up in a traditional home, and had a difficult time believing her daughter was a lesbian.

"Ashley accepted the fact that your mother was ignorant, and forgave her. But let's stop talking about your mother. When you come to New York, give me a call so I can take you to the restaurant. By the way, do you even like Ethiopian food?"

"I love Ethiopian food. What did you guys have to eat?"

"The food is tantalizing, and each time we went there, we always overstuffed ourselves. We usually ordered appetizers before our main course. I am a vegetarian and tried to get your sister to give up eating meat, but she refused. Ashley had the Meat Sambusa, and I ate the Vegetable Sambusa. Ashley selected a dish called Yebeg Alicha Fitfit for her main course, which is tender lamb cooked in butter with onions and peppers, and I had Yater Kikalicha; split peas cooked and seasoned with onions, peppers, and herbs. When you come back to New York, let me know so I can take you there.

"After dinner, we came back to her apartment and watched old movies while holding each other. As I relive these moments, I sometimes wonder if she were alive would we still be together."

"I am glad you and Ashley were able to spend time together. Unfortunately, I did not get an opportunity to see her. The last time we spoke, I told her to hurry up and pack so we could go to Las Vegas to escape the wrath of my demented husband and his mistress. I will forever blame myself for her murder. It was my fault for marrying and staying with Mark. Ashley told me to leave him years ago, but I was too hardheaded."

"Sonia, these last few years have been difficult for me and you. I just hope one day you will learn how to forgive yourself. I am not sure how to tell you this, but I must. I met a special someone six months ago, and we are moving on to the next level. I am leaving Ashley's apartment and moving into a three-story brownstone in the Carroll Gardens section of Brooklyn. Ashley kept a diary and I didn't want to take it with me, so I will send it to you."

"Thanks for preserving Ashley's memories for us. I am surprised

Ashley kept a diary. Please send it right away. I can't wait to begin reading it. I am so happy for you, Samantha. Tell me more about your new home and partner."

"The previous owners renovated the brownstone last year back to its original state. The integrity of the building was preserved and the updates are modern. The beige-colored crown moldings complement the pink-salmon colored walls and the mahogany wood floors. I don't know if Ashley told you how much I love to cook, and this kitchen was custom-made for me. The kitchen has a huge island made of mahogany wood and rose-colored marble tile flooring. There are two one-bedroom apartments on the second and third floors that I am going to rent out."

"While growing up, Ashley and I always talked about buying a brownstone when we got older, so I am sure she is smiling down on you right now. Now, tell me about your new special friend."

"Karen and I met at the Starbucks on 125th Street in Harlem, New York. I had gone out dancing the night before and was suffering from a bad hangover. Ashley never liked going to gay bars, but I find them to be comforting, if you know what I mean. When I walked in, Karen was drinking a White Chocolate Caffe Mocha, while reading the Business section of the New York Times. I first noticed her smooth, flawless, pecan complexion and long, reddish-brown locs. It took me awhile to approach her, but when she looked up at me with those dreamy, brown eyes, I walked over and asked her name. We talked for hours and spent the rest of the day with each other. She is a real estate broker in Brooklyn and helped me find the property I bought. Meeting her saved my life, as she helped me to realize I had a right to be happy and to love again. As the saying goes, people come into your life for a reason, a season, or a lifetime.

"When Ashley and I first met, I was going through a bitter divorce and battle over my son, and through her wisdom and encouraging words, I was able to overcome it. My family and friends told me that I was insane for moving into Ashley's apartment and fighting your mother over her belongings. They told me to let go of the past and move on, but how could I move on? When Ashley died, a part of me died with her, and I am only alive today because I have her memories. You would not believe it, but Ashley's clothes and shoes were still in the closet and the suitcase she was packing remained open. Her apartment was like a mausoleum. I kept everything the same, and you could still see remnants of blood on the walls.

"When Karen came into my life, she helped me sort through Ashley's clothing and paintings. We gave her clothing and shoes to a shelter for battered women, and her paintings went to Momo, her best friend. Karen has been patient with me, and I find myself in love once again. I fall in love easily, and open to the possibilities. Oh, I forgot to tell you that Momo moved back to New York after her divorce."

"I didn't know Momo got a divorce. I've been out of touch with Ashley's friends. I am sorry to hear that. What happened?"

"According to Momo, her husband got old and boring. She was running away from a lot of people when they married. She took Desmond's death really hard and was trying to reacquaint with her mother before she died. Anyway, she eventually finished law school and now works for New York City's Board of Education."

"I am glad to hear Momo is doing well. When you speak to her again, tell her that I said hello. It is always a pleasure speaking to you, and I look forward to receiving Ashley's journal. By the way, thanks for putting flowers on her gravesite for me. This year, I plan to visit her for the first time," I said.

"I think you should make the trip, Sonia. You should at least see where she is resting. Three years is not a long time when it involves the mourning of a love one; it takes time. Let me know when you come to town. Take care of yourself."

I was happy for Samantha and knew we would no longer be in contact with each other. I wished her the best and thought about what I was going through presently. Moving to England gave me the opportunity to start my life over. Living in Ajani's huge mansion was a woman's dream come true. However, sometimes I feel as if I do not deserve to be alive and enjoying life while my sister is dead. After my ordeal with the men in my past, specifically Mark, Frank, Desmond, and Amadore, I needed a real break from the male species. But, when I desperately needed a place to stay, Ajani welcomed me into his home.

I didn't mean to fall in love with him; it just happened. Ajani's copper-brown complexion, dark, brown eyes, and six-foot-four muscular frame is ideal for a woman like me. When he speaks, it is like listening to the silky, smooth R&B singer Barry White, as I play back the words he said to me when I arrived at the London Heathrow airport.

"Sonia, you look so beautiful. I would never have imagined anyone would want to hurt you. You are welcome in my home, and it would please me if you would consider it your own."

Before going to England, I told myself I was going to remain celibate for at least a year, but that shit went out the window the minute I looked into his eyes. We began sleeping together two weeks after my arrival. Who would have thought we would even be a couple right now? When we first met, Tracy was more appealing to him. Tracy had him wrapped around her little finger and used him for his money. Tracy is a free spirited person who does what she wants to do, when she wants to do it, and she wasn't ready to give up her life to settle down with him. I benefited from his lavish gifts because I went along for the ride. He paid for our first trip to Europe, and boy, did we have a good time. I was jealous of Tracy's fine catch.

I still do not know what Ajani does for a living or how he earned his wealth because he doesn't share that part of his life with me. When I inquired about his work, he always changed the subject. At first, I thought he was involved with drugs or some other illegal dealings, but I have not seen evidence that confirms those suspicions. Whatever work he does, involves traveling.

It surprises me that I am still living in England, because my first plan was to stay for only one year, but love warps our judgment sometimes. Even though we are having problems, he has been an excellent father to my daughter. He wasted no time in setting up a trust fund for her and enrolling her into an impressive boarding school. So, when he asked me if he could adopt her, I agreed. When my mother found out about the boarding school, she strongly opposed it and suggested we move to Georgia.

"Sonia, I don't think it is wise for you and Jasmine to remain overseas. You are not married to him, and therefore, you are not obligated to stay with him. Don't get me wrong, I appreciate all he has done for us, but it is time for you to move on. Jasmine's father is dead, and Ajani shouldn't make decisions about her well-being. I don't trust him, Sonia," she warned.

"Why don't you trust him? Ajani thinks highly of you and was heartbroken when you left. He planned on renovating the guesthouse for you."

"Haven't you learned your lesson yet? Wasn't Ajani Tracy's boyfriend? I'm not stupid; I know you two are sleeping together. I guess you will never learn."

"First off, Tracy and Ajani broke up months ago, and Tracy is seeing someone else right now. Whether you believe me or not, I have learned my lesson, and we are not sleeping together," I said.

That was three years ago, back when I didn't want to admit we were sleeping together or reveal to her about the adoption. Sometimes mothers are psychic, and it is my fault I didn't listen to her warning about Ajani, but I couldn't avoid his charm.

Chapter 2

Mom and I speak daily now, as if she lives right around the corner and not in another country. Ashley's death taught me to put family first. I don't know how much time either of us has on earth; therefore, I'm cherishing each moment we share. Mom and I were estranged when I was teenager, so we have much catching up to do.

Today's call was a little disturbing; someone tried to break into the home she shares with Teddi. What alarmed me is the fact they live in a gated community in Alpharetta, Georgia. What is the point of living in a gated community if you could still be a victim of robbery? I remember when they first moved into their new home, because all she did was talk about how beautiful the house was and that it looked better than the house in England. Mom made sure to send me pictures of it by means of e-mail. The mansion has seven bedrooms, six bathrooms, and seven acres of beautifully landscaped land. They have three winding staircases leading to the balcony. Mom is most proud of the glass encased elevator that goes up to the third floor where the main bedroom is situated. I was happy for them.

Mom and Teddi have been together for five years and she seemed content. My biggest question to her was why they had to have all of that space. They are an older couple with no young children and only one grandchild. I am planning on visiting them in November for Thanksgiving, which is three months away.

"Sonia, I couldn't sleep last night. I know it's because I ate dinner so late. I should have known better. I always have nightmares when I eat late. Nevertheless, I couldn't resist the baked lasagna Teddi made.

"Anyway, Teddi had to work late last night, and I get jittery when he is not home. I looked out the window and noticed a car parked in our driveway. I was not expecting visitors at three o'clock in the morning, so I immediately called the cops. My first thought was Teddi left the gate unlocked, but that seemed unusual because he always locked the gate when he left.

"While waiting for the cops to arrive, the car suddenly left my driveway and went to my next-door neighbor's house. I immediately ran and got my binoculars so I could see...you know, since we live so far apart. I noticed there were three more unfamiliar cars in front of their home. I knew my neighbors were out of town, so no one should have been there. I called the police again and told them to hurry up.

"I was so afraid, Sonia. I wanted to keep them on the phone, but they had to keep their lines clear for other emergencies. They assured me the police were on their way, though. I calmed my nerves down enough to come up with a plan. I plugged in my curling iron, got out my hairspray, and grabbed Teddi's gun from underneath the bed. I ran downstairs and let man's best friend, Niro, out of his cage, and then ran back upstairs to look out the window again. What I saw made me afraid for my life.

"There were six to ten guys getting out of their cars with black hoodies on. They broke off into different directions, with two of them headed in my direction. I tried not to scream as I dialed the police again. The operator on the line tried to keep me calm. She told me to find a hiding place inside the house until the police arrived. I took my weapons with me as I hid in the attic. I made it there just in time as I heard them break the glass window in the living room. As soon as those motherfuckers entered my house, Niro grabbed one of their legs, preventing him from going upstairs. The other perpetrator tried to get Niro off his partner, but Niro locked onto the guy's legs.

"It seemed like forever for the cops to get here. When they finally arrived, Niro still had the perpetrator's leg in his mouth, while the other tried to escape out of the broken window. I was so lucky to have escaped injury. The police told me one of my neighbors got shot in the back while trying to escape through his back door. I told Teddi we have to move because I can't live in this house any longer. But he told me that he will install another camera and get another dog."

"Mom, I am so glad to hear you are okay, because I don't know what I would do if something happened to you. Thank God you were not harmed. Why don't you come back to Europe for a few weeks? You know Ajani wants you to come back."

"No, honey, I am fine. Besides, you know how I feel about Ajani. I don't trust him, and I would prefer not to be in his presence right now. How is Ajani doing by the way?" she asked.

"Ajani is fine, I guess. We've been having some difficulties. We act like an old married couple, with all the bickering we've been doing lately. We've been sleeping in separate bedrooms for the last two months."

"I'm sorry to hear that. The last time we spoke, you were fantasizing about getting married to him."

"Well, I found out good ol' Ajani has been seeing a woman named Chelsea for at least six months, perhaps longer. He even bought a condo for her on Central Park East in New York."

"Now you know why I don't trust him. I told you there was something about him that I didn't like. Didn't I tell you not to trust him?"

"I hate to admit it, Mom, but you were right about him, and I should have listened to you. Don't worry about me, though. You have enough to worry about right now."

"You are my daughter, and I will always worry about you. I think you need to leave him and come back to the United States. You and Jasmine can stay with us. Save yourself the trouble and heartache by moving on."

"When I confronted him about her, he said he would stop seeing her immediately. Part of me wants to leave him, but I don't want to disrupt Jasmine's life right now. She is doing well in school and has many friends. She is close to Ajani and considers him her father."

"But, he is not her father. Why would you stay with a man who cheats on you? I don't understand you, Sonia. What makes you pick these types of men? It's like you're a glutton for punishment. Don't you deserve respect? I think I know the reason you've decided to stay. You are enjoying his wealth. Ajani has proved to you that he cannot be faithful to you, but you remain with him. Haven't you learned you can't force someone to love you?"

"Mom, Ajani adopted Jasmine three years ago, so he is legally her father. And how long did it take you to leave, Daddy? You stayed with him even though he was verbally abusive to you. The love I have for Ajani is real and is not going to go away overnight. I'm not sure I'm ready to give up on him."

"Why are you comparing yourself to me? I was wrong for staying with your father as long as I did, which means you should have learned from my past mistakes. After your father and I split, I had a difficult time trusting men and had low self-esteem. I know how difficult it is for you, and don't want you to experience what your father put me through. You'll make the right decision for you when the time comes. I'm here if you need me, Sonia. I'll talk to you later."

I know my mother means well and is thinking about my well-being, but she doesn't understand the complexity of my situation.

Chapter 3

I received Ashley's journal today. At first, I was afraid to open it, but knew I had to read it. Since I held my sister in such high regard, I feared I would find out stuff that would change my opinion of her. Still, I proceeded to read Ashley's first entry.

November 11, 1987

Dear Diary,

I am so excited. I met someone special today, and her name is Amber Donella Williams. Amber is one year older than I. She is sixteen years old and beautiful. This was the first time I've been attracted to a girl. When she kissed me, it felt so right and natural. I am a little confused by my feelings and don't know what to do about them. I don't want anyone to know about what happened. My mother and father would kill me if they found out. I wish I could share this wonderful experience with Sonia, but she is so caught up with Mark. He is the only one she cares about right now. Amber told me we should keep our special kiss a secret, because if people knew about it, they would tease us. People already teased me about being a tomboy, so I can handle it. I am glad we met, because she understands me in ways no one else can.

Signing off!

Understand you! So, it appears Ashley was leading a secret life from the beginning. I always wondered how she got into girls.

I remember when we used to watch college basketball on T.V. and fantasize about the different players. My favorite team was North Carolina's Tar Heels and my husband-to-be was Rick Fox. Ashley favored Georgetown's Hoyas and her husband-to-be was Reggie Williams.

It felt funny reading Ashley's journal. The pain of not having her with me right now is so unbearable. Wouldn't it be great if there was a machine that could go back in time? If one existed, I would be the first in line to change the way I treated her when we were teenagers, and perhaps I could have saved her life. Ashley was right when she said I didn't have time for her.

It was especially hard reading about her feelings for Amber, whom I barely remember meeting. I would have never suspected they were a couple. I did think Amber was a little different, with her multiple piercings and tattoos all over her body. She wore her jet black hair in a Mohawk with the sides shaved. I think she was what they called Gothic. She looked ghastly in her black clothing, ruby-red lipstick, and black fingernail polish. It was strange to see a black girl dressed that way. I tried not to judge her too much, though, because she was Ashley's best friend.

When Ashley finally came out to our parents, I remember how difficult it was for her, but I felt they needed to know. I will forever feel responsible for forcing her to talk to them and causing that pain in her life. Mom never trusted Amber because she was too abrasive and disrespectful.

After a deep sigh, I continued reading the journal.

November 13, 1987

Dear Diary,

Amber and I went to 42nd Street today to play video games and drink alcohol. We snuck into the movie theater and drank Pink Champale while watching a porno movie. At first, I was a little shy about the whole encounter, but the buzz from the Champale put me at ease. While watching the action taking place on the screen, Amber and I embraced in a passionate kiss as she inserted her finger into my vagina. I was overcome with great pleasure, and immediately fell in love with Amber. My body came alive for the first time, and I didn't know what was happening to me. I hope we remain friends forever. I didn't want the day to end, but I knew if I didn't get home on time, Mom would have a bird.

Signing off!

November 27, 1987

Dear Diary,

Mom invited everyone over for Thanksgiving. Auntie Cora just came back from Germany where she lived for the last seven years. She's Mom's youngest sister. Auntie Cora did not have children, but she sure had several male friends. Her new boyfriend, Samuel, is a light-skinned version of Denzel Washington, which equals fine. My grandmother came up from Chicago, and she looked so good. We haven't seen her in years because of the stroke she had four years ago. Mom also introduced us to her new boyfriend, Smitty. He looks like a player to me, with his dark, cocoa brown skin and processed, wavy hair. Mom can do much better than him and should stay away from pretty boys. Daddy stopped by for a few minutes and, of course, had a nice, young-looking woman on his arm. She looked like she was in her early twenties. I couldn't tell what her nationality was, but I think she was Latina. Mom cooked up a storm. I sure hope I'll be able to cook like her when I get older. Mom is a good cook and didn't disappoint with her hefty-sized portions of: turkey with cornbread stuffing, collard greens, green beans, seafood gumbo with extra King crab legs, peas and rice, pot roast with red potatoes, sweet potato pie, pumpkin pie, banana pudding with whipped cream, and a chocolate mousse cake. I enjoyed spending time with our family, but the feeling quickly disappeared when I called Amber and found out she was in Juvenile Hall for

17

stealing a pair of pants from the Gap. I am going to miss her, and wonder how I'm going to have fun without her. I wish Sonia didn't hang around that stupid boyfriend so much.

Signing off!

December 4, 1987

Dear Diary,

Pink Champale was calling my name today. So, I decided to leave school early to buy a bottle, and almost bumped into Sonia and Mark as they were heading out the back door. I waited until they walked down the block, and then I went in the opposite direction. I wonder where they were running off to. I enjoy drinking because it helps me forget about the shit I'm dealing with at home. My mother has been a pain in the ass since Sonia moved in with Daddy. Mom told me that Sonia is a traitor because she knew how badly my father treated her. Sonia thinks Mom is bitter about Daddy leaving her for a younger woman. Mom is not bitter. Dad was abusive and disrespectful. The only reason Sonia likes living with him is because he's not keeping a close eye on her.

As soon as I got my bottle of Champale, I hopped on the number 5 train, headed downtown to 42nd Street, and snuck in to see another porno movie. I sat next to a white man who was jacking off and thought about leaving, but couldn't move. He looked at me as he released a load of white slimy shit from his dick. He asked me if I wanted to taste it. I told him hell no. He grabbed me by my head and put his nasty, stinking dick in my mouth. It tasted salty and slimy, and I thought I was going to die. He forced me to suck his dick until it grew again in size. I couldn't believe it. As I sucked his dick, he fingered me and I started to cum. It didn't feel like when Amber did it; it felt better. He grabbed me by my hair and took me to the men's bathroom. I did not expect to see people having sex in there. He pushed me into one of the stalls and bent me over. He entered me with such force I screamed. He told me to shut the fuck up and stuck his dick into my mouth to ensure my silence. I cried and cried while he came inside of my mouth. The sick part about this shit is I had mixed *emotions behind what happened to me. Was I raped? I enjoyed it so much that it must mean I was an active participant. This creep told me that he enjoyed being with me and gave me fifty dollars for my time. He told me if I wanted to get more money, he would see me next week at the same time. Even though I knew he raped me and it was not my fault, I still felt like a cheap whore. A part of me felt I got what I deserved because I should have been in school. After he left, I stayed in the stall for a few minutes to get myself together, because if my mother saw me looking like this, she would kill me. Thanks to Sonia, my mother thought I was a whore anyway.*

I hope Amber doesn't have to stay locked up for long, or else I am going to lose my mind.

I cut my wrist the other day, and it helped soothe some of the pain I've been feeling in my heart. I only bled a little bit, so I just put a Band-Aid on it. I'll wear long sleeves to school tomorrow so no one will see the scar.

Signing off!

I am so angry right now. Ashley should have told me what happened to her. I would have had the bastard arrested and carted off to jail. The tears streamed down my face as I reread this entry in her diary. I remember that period in her life and noticed a slight change in her.

"I am so sorry, Ashley, for not being there for you. You were crying out for my help, and I was too selfish to hear you. Please forgive me," I screamed.

It was three o' clock in the morning, and I couldn't put the journal down. I had to read a few more entries.

December 5, 1987

Dear Diary,

I am a little depressed today. I can't believe the fucker raped me. When I got home and thought about what happened to me, I cut my wrist again to ease the pain. I almost cut a vein yesterday, and had a hard time stopping the blood. I don't want to die, but I don't know how to stop the pain in my heart. I have to control my emotions. A small part of me wants to go back to the movie theater and beat the shit out of that man.

A letter from Amber arrived today, and I couldn't stop smiling. I felt sorry for her as I read how much she hated Juvenile Hall. She tried to escape, and they told her if she tried to do that again, they would add two more months onto her sentence. I highlighted the sentence where she said she missed me and couldn't wait to see me again. I was so happy to hear from her. I thought she forgot about me.

Signing off!

December 9, 1987

Dear Diary,

I don't know what came over me today, I had a strong urge to return to the movie theater. A part of me was hoping I would run into my attacker so I could ram my fist down his throat. As soon as I entered, I scanned the place for him, but he wasn't there, so I took a seat next to a couple who was making out. I had my bottle of Champale with me and I drank until my heart was content, while watching the screen and the couple next to me. Boredom quickly overcame me, so I went to the women's bathroom to see what was going on in there. When I opened the door, there was a serious orgy going on. I felt the urge to join them, when I noticed an older man sniffing a white powder-like substance in the corner. He offered me some and I figured what the hell. Within minutes, the old geezer began to look appealing to me, and it didn't take long for me to want to go down on him. The powder made me think I was invincible at sucking dick, and of course, I felt I should be compensated for my good deed. I took his shit out of my mouth and made him beg for me to put it back in. I told him he had to pay for my services. He tried to give me twenty-five dollars, which I declined. He eventually whipped out one hundred dollars, and I told him it still wasn't enough. So, he gave me two hundred, and that's when I allowed him to cum in my mouth. After he released, I left his old ass gasping for air and went on to the next client, who was going down on a woman. I watched them *for a few minutes and then decided to pull his dick out of his pants and suck it to my satisfaction. I must have been doing a good job, because he stopped what he was doing with the woman and concentrated on me. The woman was not to be outdone, so she started sucking my shit. I thought I was going to lose my fucking mind. I participated in a threesome just like in the movies. I came down from my high, but wanted more. Sue, the girl who blew my mind, gave me some more powder to sniff. Sue is twenty- one years old, and told me she makes money selling dope and her body. She asked me if I wanted to make some serious money because she knew where. I didn't mind getting paid for my work, but what interested me most was the sex, so I declined. I needed to get home before my mother did, or else she would kill me.*

Signing off!

I couldn't believe what I was reading. My little sister did not know what she was doing because she was too young. I could kill Amber, and if I saw that bitch on the street right now, I would fuck her up. Ashley did a superb job keeping her life secret. My parents would flip the fuck out if they knew what she was doing.

✿✿

Ajani came home early tonight, stating he wanted to talk about our future. We did not have a future, and I would let him know that.

"Sonia, we need to talk. I don't like arguing with you, and I want us to work this out. There is a lot I have to apologize for, and just hope you can forgive me."

"What is there to talk about? Aren't you tired of apologizing to me? Ajani, you have cheated on me with several women, and each time, you asked for forgiveness. If you want to spend the rest of your life with Chelsea, you do not need my permission."

"Chelsea and I have been friends for years before we took it to the next level. You and I were so compatible at first, and I was convinced we would get married one day. But I never told you we would be seeing each other exclusively."

"No, we never discussed the extent of our courtship, but assumed since we were living and sleeping together, we were a couple."

"I'm sorry about not making myself clear to you. You knew before you came to live with me the kind of man I was. How long did Tracy and I see each other? Not long, because I was a bachelor and enjoyed it."

"If that were the case, why did you feel it necessary to apologize every time you got caught cheating? You didn't owe me an explanation if we were not a couple."

"I am a gentleman, and it was the right thing to do at the time."

"You are so full of it, Ajani. You knew what you were doing. Our relationship was one-sided, and it was in your favor."

"What do you mean? You could have dated other people if you wanted. I never told you not to."

"I see what game you're playing, and it's not going to work. What do you want from me, Ajani? If you would like me to move out, let me know."

"I don't want you to move. I want us to get married. We can't change the past, but we can work toward the future."

"Are you smoking crack? You want me to marry you, why? What about Chelsea?"

"We are no longer seeing each other. I told her that I wanted to be with you exclusively."

"How did she take the news? I'm sure she thought you bumped your head."

"She thinks you're a gold-digger and that you could never make me happy."

"My name is not Tracy. Why would she think that about me?"

"All of my friends feel that way. They said you should have gone back to the United States a long time ago."

"You must have felt the same way, since you never took me around them. Are you ashamed of me?"

"No, I am not ashamed of you, but I knew my friends didn't like you. So, it didn't make sense for you to be around them. At some point, I realized I was no longer happy being with Chelsea and looked forward to spending more time with you. I've watched you mature into a sensible and intelligent woman. Please do not be offended. It is just I looked at you through different colored lenses."

"You have made me look like a fool too many times, and I can't see myself marrying someone I can't trust. I've gone down this path before, and it's time for me to go in a different direction," I said.

"Give us a chance, Sonia. I will show you how much you mean to me. You will be my wife one day, you'll see. Let's go to St. Tropez for the holidays. Call your mother to see if she wants to go with us."

"Ajani, I need some time away from you. Do you think a vacation is going to change my mind? Besides, I have already arranged to visit my mother in Georgia. So, you should go and spend some time alone to get your head together. Every time you cheated, you put a hole in my heart, and I can't keep putting a Band-Aid on it. I have a lot to think about, and I don't know if I want to continue seeing you. I gave you several opportunities to treat me with respect, and you didn't."

"I understand what you are saying, but still want you to give me another opportunity to make it up to you. Why don't we visit your mother for Christmas? The villa has more than enough room to hold your friends and family members. The villa has eight bedrooms, nine bathrooms, and a heated pool which overlooks Ramatuelle Bay and Canoubiers Bay. The servant's quarters and the tennis courts are the last areas needing renovation. The contractor assured me that the villa will be ready for us by Thanksgiving, and I was hoping you would help me decorate. I know you are going to fall in love with the magnificent view and the many gardens on the property."

"Ajani, you have provided me with the life I have only seen in movies. I wake up pinching myself because I feel as if I'm dreaming. Still, I blame myself for putting you on a pedestal and making you out to be more than you are. I am sorry, Ajani, I've made other plans. Enjoy your trip."

I am so proud of myself for standing firm in my decision. He is right about one thing, and that is I *have* matured. The only reason I allowed him to adopt Jasmine was to ensure her future, since her real father is dead and didn't have insurance that would help take care of her.

Ajani is so fucking predictable, and I am finally tired of playing these same games with him. Quite frankly, it is getting boring. Every time he feels guilty about his actions, he buys another home or car. With Ms. Switzerland, he bought me a Mediterranean-styled house in Santa Barbara, California. Because I threatened to leave him, he put the house in my name. He said it was time I owned property of my own. Who does he think he is fooling? I don't even get a chance to spend time there.

I've made up my mind. I am leaving this man, and moving on to bigger and better opportunities. It's time for a little vacation and to give my friend Tracy a call. We haven't spoken in about three months, and I miss her. It's time for me to get gully again.

Chapter 4

"What's going on? We haven't spoken in awhile. Tell me what's going on with you, mi amiga."

"All is good, Sonia. I was just thinking about calling you. Ashley's been on my mind lately, and I still can't believe she's gone. Sheila and I broke up two days ago, and I need a place to stay. How are you and Ajani doing?"

"You know, same old shit, just a different day. He admitted to seeing a woman named Chelsea. I didn't even catch him this time; he told me on his own."

"What point was he trying to make by being honest this time? Where is he taking you now to make up for his indiscretions? I know where, the South of France. He is so damn predictable. Aren't you tired of being his doormat?"

"Yeah, the bastard offered to take me to the St. Tropez for Thanksgiving. But, I told him no because I made other plans. He is renovating the villa he bought last year. If it were different circumstances, I would have jumped at the chance to go, but I have to stand for something. He told me that his friends don't like me and think I am a gold-digger."

"You are a gold-digger. Why are you still living in England? The answer is that you enjoy spending his money. Be honest!"

"I am not a gold-digger, Tracy. I have feelings for him. True, it is hard to pick between the extravagant lifestyle his money provides me and leaving him for good. I've traveled all over the world and experienced so many wonderful things that are unbelievable for someone like me. Still, I'm tired of feeling like a fool."

"What do you mean *someone like you*? You deserve to be taken care of, too. Do you think because you grew up in the hood you deserve less? You must be crazy."

"You're right. We all know how I grew up, and it's my turn to get the best out of life. I think he was ashamed of me because I didn't grow up with money. It seems as if Chelsea is well-off. And guess what? He had the nerve to propose to me and think I would accept it. I don't intend on walking away from him empty-handed, though. Girl, he bought me a house in Santa Barbara, California," I said with a chuckle.

"You go, girl. I'm glad to hear you finally listened to me. You are where you need to be, and I wouldn't leave him right now. Who cares if he creeps every now and again? Enjoy the moment. You dealt with Mark's cheating ways, and he couldn't and didn't leave you with squat. I think you should sell the property Ajani bought you so you can get some fast cash."

"Tracy, I shouldn't be surprised by your response, but I'm tired of feeling like a doormat. Money isn't everything, Tracy. As a college-educated woman, I can take care of myself. I want more from him, and he can't seem to give it to me. Mark was poor and crazy as hell, but at one time, we loved each other. I would take love and respect over money any day. So what happened between you and Sheila? I'm sorry to hear you are no longer together."

"Sheila is an extraordinary person and an awesome friend, but she wants something from me I can't give her. You know the bitch asked me to marry her? I want to get married one day, but it will not be to a woman."

"New York does not allow same sex marriages, so you couldn't get married anyway."

"The bitch is crazy, and I would never even consider marrying a woman. I will miss her, though. By the way, I'm seeing a younger guy by the name of Devan, and he is sexy as all hell. He is the only man I've been with in two years, and I miss being with men."

"Devan must be fine if he has you thinking about settling down. Tell me more about him."

"He is not the reason I want to settle down. Devan is twenty-two years old and fun to hang out with. I don't know if he is the one, but he does have me thinking about my future. We met six months ago at a bar. He is a construction worker and college student. It was hard to resist his double-dimpled face and thin frame. He is a talented lover and often makes my toes curl."

"I miss you. When are you coming out here?"

"Right now, I need to concentrate on moving out of Sheila's house. Before I forget to tell you, Alike and I had dinner last week. She told me I could move into her apartment if I needed to, and I think I'm going to take her up on the offer."

"I didn't realize you and Alike were still in contact with each other. Why don't you visit us in England until you make your decision? I'll have Ajani send you a ticket before he heads out to Miami Beach. He is buying a club there."

"Wow, Miami Beach. Don't tell me you will finally make it back to the States. Miami is a great hotspot. Ajani is forever the businessman. Is he a real estate investor?"

"He *is* an investor, and has been for quite a few years. I've been checking out some houses online, and found an eight-bedroom estate on Star Island Drive. If he buys this place, I will not leave him," I chuckled.

"I wonder where he got the initial start-up money. Did his parents have money?"

"He used to be a vice president of a bank in London, and eventually got into real estate investing."

"The place sounds beautiful, but where in the hell is Star Island? I never even heard of it."

"You're so funny. It's near South Beach. Ajani is going to take a look at it when he closes on the nightclub. If I decide to stay with him, I'll ask him to find and lease retail space for a boutique. I miss working."

"Sonia, I'm not convinced this man started his career in banking. Vice presidents do not make that much money, but then again, who said he was an honest employee. Did he tell you what bank he used to work for?"

"Why are you skeptical, Tracy? What difference does it make where he got his money? I didn't ask to see his resume. All I know is he owns commercial and residential properties throughout the world. The man is wealthy, and who cares how he got his money? By the way, I've been meaning to ask you about your place of employment. Where are you working again?

"You know darn well what I do for a living. I am a kept woman, and Sheila has done an excellent job of taking care of me."

"Tracy, are you sorry you let Ajani slip away?" I inquired

"Sometimes I think about him and wonder what it would be like if I chose to stay with him. His friends would be well within their rights for calling me a gold-digger. I'm not ashamed about demanding money for my time. Ajani wanted me to change, and I couldn't do that for him. You can't change a whore into a housewife. But let's not belabor the issue about Ajani. As long as you are comfortable with how he earns his living, then it's okay with me. Just be careful."

"Is there something you're not telling me? Ajani told me that he saw Alike on his last trip to New York. Did Alike say anything to you? She must have, so you might as well tell me. If not, then it would be best for you to mind your business, Tracy."

"I didn't know Alike saw Ajani, because she never mentioned it to me. You're right. I need to mind my business, so I'll drop the subject. I don't want to get you upset with me."

"Thanks, I appreciate your concern for me, though. So how is Alike doing? I haven't been good at keeping in touch with her. I need to give her a call."

"Alike's dating and escort business is doing real well. You wouldn't believe her transformation. She looks like a million bucks with her new hairstyle. She lost some weight and let her hair grow. She wears her hair pinned up most of the time. According to her, she has found the love of her life, and they are getting married next year. His name is David, and he is an entertainment lawyer she met in drug rehab."

"Girlfriend is doing her thing, and I ain't mad at her. As we already know, there are a lot of men willing to pay to be with her. Have they set a wedding date?"

"They're getting married in June of next year. You should see how happy she looks."

"Great! I am so happy for her. I can't believe she didn't mention Ajani at least once."

"You are persistent for someone who just told me they were going to leave him. She just told me that Ajani had a lot of secrets and was not trustworthy. She expressed her love for him and wondered why you were still with him. Has he ever been violent with you? Alike stated he could be verbally and physically abusive."

"No, he has never hit me. He has abused me mentally, though, with all the different women he has paraded around town with. Ajani told me the only reason they broke up was because they abused drugs, which would account for his mistreating her."

"There is never a justification for abuse, Sonia. Did you know he was married before? Alike said his first wife died during childbirth. Alike found a picture of a beautiful young woman, and when she questioned him about it, he brutally beat her."

"He never mentioned having a wife. Did Alike find out anything about this woman?"

"Alike was hospitalized for a month after the beating."

"Oh my God! Why did he beat her for asking a simple question?"

"Charles, his driver, saved her life when he stopped Ajani. He took her to the hospital and held vigil by her bedside until she recovered. He then told her who the young woman was and what she meant to Ajani. Ajani met her in Belize when she was fourteen years old. Her name was Antolina, and she was from the Garínagu tribe. She died two years later during childbirth. According to Alike's description, she was breathtaking with her long, straight, black hair, slanted, coal black eyes, and strong African features. Charles told Alike that Antolina was the love of Ajani's life, and when she died, it changed him into an unloving and uncaring human being. Alike finally understood why Ajani never proposed to her, even though they lived together for six years."

"I didn't realize they were together so long. Did she move back in with Ajani after she came out of the hospital? And what happened to the baby?"

"Alike moved into Charles' apartment, and the baby died with his mother."

"What Charles did was honorable. I'm going to have to confront Ajani about this new revelation, and let's hope he doesn't get violent. I'm not Alike; I will kick his ass."

"Why would you confront him about this? If he wants to show you how much you mean to him, then he needs to prove he is trustworthy. Let him tell you about his life, and if he does, then you know he is serious about spending the rest of his life with you."

"That is some good advice. A part of me wants to believe him this time, and it is possible he means it this time. Let me tell you about the time I picked up his private line while he was in the bathroom. The person on the other end was adamant about speaking to Ajani right away, and did not want to leave a message for him. He told me to tell Ajani it would be in his best interest to stop avoiding his calls. I told him to hold on while I went to get Ajani. When I told Ajani he had a phone call, you could tell he wanted to curse me out for answering his phone in the first place, but he remained calm. I knew I was being trifling, but my nosey nature got the best of me. I apologized for answering the phone and immediately left the room because I didn't want to hear his mouth. I didn't go too far, though, because I wanted to know what was going on. So, I went into the room adjacent to his office, put a glass to the wall, and listened to his conversation. Ajani was so heated that all I could hear was him screaming at the poor man. He told the man that if he did not do what was expected of him, he would be eternally sorry. He fired the man and told him that Charles would cut him a check for his services."

"Alike told me how shrewd and maniacal he can be, and that he has a low toleration for incompetence. You can't be a man of his wealth and be too kind, I guess."

"You and I both know that Alike is still in love with him."

"You know my feelings about love, and it has nothing to do with anything. They were together for six years, so I'm sure she still has *some* feelings for him. You know the deal. You were in love with Mark, and what did loving him do for your life? Not a damn thing. He caused you misery and pain. So what are you going to do about Ajani's proposal? I know he hurt you, but sometimes, you have to make decisions in life you don't agree with. If marrying him means you get to live your dreams, then just go ahead and marry him, as long as you don't have to sign a prenuptial agreement."

"I'm sure he will insist I sign on the dotted line. He's not a stupid man and I don't have a problem signing, as long as I benefit financially in some way. Tracy, we have been on this phone for four hours. I think you need to make a trip out to England, because it is obvious we have a lot to talk about.

"Before we hang up, I almost forgot to tell you about Ashley's partner. She is moving out of Ashley's old apartment. She also sent me Ashley's diary, and I've found out some interesting details about my dear sister."

"About fucking time that bitch moved out. How long has Ashley been dead? She should have moved on awhile ago. I hope she didn't say anything about me in her diary," Tracy stated.

"Well, Tracy, I have some errands to run, so we'll talk soon."

I forgot how insensitive Tracy could be sometimes. She has a heart of stone.

Chapter 5

"Ajani, Tracy and I had a long conversation yesterday. I suggested she come and stay with us for awhile. I hope you don't mind. By the way, what's going on with the nightclub in Miami? Are you going to buy it? I hope so, because I would like to open up a women's clothing boutique there. Let me know when you're going so I can go with you and scope out some possible areas."

"I'll talk to my realtor and have her find some areas for you to look at. You can go with me to Miami next time because I have a few other stops to make before returning here to England."

"Where else are you going? I would like to take a look at the club and some homes."

"I'm going to New York first, and then I have a two-day meeting in Boston before going to Florida. So will Sheila be with Tracy, and when do they want to come? Let me know so I can arrange the flight," Ajani said, changing the subject.

"Sheila and Tracy are no longer seeing each other, and Tracy hasn't decided on when she wants to come out here. She's dating a young man named Devan."

"Tracy is seeing men again? How interesting. When did this happen? The last time I spoke to Alike, she told me Tracy was still living with Sheila."

"When was the last time you spoke to Alike? I didn't know you were keeping tabs on Tracy."

"I'm not keeping tabs on Tracy, Sonia. The last time I spoke to Alike was when I went to New York a few months ago. Didn't I tell you this already? Maybe you *should* go to Miami for a little vacation. Why don't you ask Tracy or your mother to go with you?"

"I think it will be a better idea to invite someone to go with me to California instead of Miami. I don't want to be a burden to you. Besides, I haven't had the opportunity to spend time there since you purchased the house."

"Call Tracy and tell her to meet you there, and I'll pay for it. Tracy is such a carefree person, that knows how to have a good time, and doesn't have any hang-ups. Let me know what you want to do."

"What in the hell do you mean she doesn't have any hang-ups? Are you reminiscing about the old days? If you miss her so much, I'll ask her to meet you in Miami."

"Sonia, you need to grow up. I'm not a perfect man, but when you needed me to step in and be the father Jasmine never had, I did it with no problem. When you and your family needed a safe place to live, I provided that, too. What about all the things I did for you? I've given you a life fit for a queen, and yet, you are still dissatisfied. You are interrogating me like I'm a common criminal. I am not going to subject myself to this bullshit anymore. If you are so unhappy living here with me, then you can leave. And you don't have to worry about money for Jasmine, because I'll continue to support her."

"I agree you have given us the perfect lifestyle, and I am forever grateful. If you want me to leave, I'll leave. I will not remain somewhere I am not wanted."

"I did not say I didn't want you to stay, Sonia. I fucked up again, and I am sorry, but I don't want you to beat me over the head about my indiscretions. I'm so tired of arguing with you, and that's why I seek comfort from other women. There are many things I need to work on, and I'm willing do that for you. I'm going to New York tomorrow morning and will not be back for two weeks. While we are apart, you need to consider whether or not you want to stay with me."

He gave me the opportunity to walk out of this relationship, but I clammed up and felt like kicking myself. Deep down inside, I know he still has feelings for Tracy and possibly Alike. I guess I should have expected that since they were both intimately involved with him.

I can't worry about Ajani right now. I need some alone time, so I will not invite Tracy to go with me to California. Since I haven't seen my father in awhile, I'll invite him to visit me instead.

"Hey, Papi, how are you doing? You've been on my mind a lot this week. I miss you."

"I'm hanging in there, Sonia. I'm so glad you called. I'm always a wreck around the time of your sister's birthday. I'm now taking Zoloft for depression. Tina and the children left me two months ago. That bitch has a lot of fucking nerve taking my children with her tired ass. She knows how much they mean to me and the pain I'm dealing with since Ashley was killed. Your abuela told me that I should have never married that whore in the first place because she was only after my money. I guess that's what I get for marrying a stripper."

"Papi, I'm sorry to hear about your troubles. The purpose of my call is to invite you to spend some time with me in California. I can arrange a flight for you tomorrow, if you like. And where did Tina go? I would like to stay in touch with the kids."

"Thanks, Sonia, but I must decline. I'm not in a good mood and would spoil everything. Tina's friend told me that she's going to file for a divorce, and I know she's going to try and take every penny. I will never allow her to bankrupt me, so I'm going to sell the house in New Jersey and move to Puerto Rico."

"Papi, you have not changed one bit. I can't believe you're going to sell the house right under Tina's nose. Don't forget about your children. They don't need to suffer because the two of you can't get along. When you and Mommy broke up, Ashley and I suffered. If you love your children, you should want to do the best for them."

"I *will* provide for my children, but that bitch did not buy this house and shouldn't benefit from my hard work. I know I've been a horrible father, and I'm sorry. I want you to know that you girls meant the world to me. Your mother accused me of being a selfish man, and I've grappled with that notion for years. I never considered myself a selfish person, but I am. I was selfish with my time and money. When I married Tina, it was to last forever, and it disturbs me that she would leave me because I am having a meltdown. Your mother would have remained by my side. Boy, do I regret the pain I caused her. I realize that what I'm going through right now is payback for what I've done to others."

"It is unfortunate you can't turn back the hands of time, but you can make sure Tina has what she needs to provide for your children."

"You know, I see Ashley in my dreams. I even find myself talking to her aloud, where other people can hear me. Last year, Tina found me in our bedroom unconscious after I swallowed a bottle of pain killers. She told me that she was so afraid and never wanted to experience that again. She thought I was dead. I promised her that I would never try to take my life again, but I broke it six months ago when I slit my wrist. Sonia, I feel so guilty for not making peace with Ashley before she got killed. Tina and the children are my world, and I can't live without them. Your abuela suggested that I move back to Puerto Rico until I can get myself together. I don't tell you this enough, but I want you to know how much I love you."

"Do you want me to work with the realtor? I think it would be best for you to leave as soon as possible because you sound stressed."

"That's a good idea. I am trying hard not to lose my mind. I have hired a realtor already, so I will need to grant you legal permission."

"Great. I'll make your flight arrangements for you, too. When would you like to leave?" I inquired.

"I have a lot of packing to do, so I guess I will be ready to leave Friday of next week."

"Papi, I can pack your belongings for you. Pack your essentials, and I will send the rest to storage or charity, whichever you prefer. I'll fly into New Jersey tomorrow and take care of you, Papi."

"Thank you, baby. I appreciate all you're doing for me. I look forward to seeing you tomorrow."

My father was there for me when I needed him, so it was my turn to be there for him. He had a lot to be guilty for, but he doesn't deserve to be miserable. How can he blame himself for Ashley's death? It was my fault. I caused her death. If I would have listened to Mom and stayed away from Mark, my sister would be alive today. I hope he finds peace in Puerto Rico. I have a strong feeling once he goes home, I will not see him again.

Before retiring to bed, I needed to unwind a bit, so I grabbed a couple of candles, a glass of wine, and proceeded to read Ashley's journal.

December 17, 1987

Dear Diary,

Amber called me last week and told me that she was going to be coming home on December 15th. At first, I was excited about the idea, but that quickly changed when we saw each other yesterday. We met at the pizza shop, and I was surprised to see how different she looked. Amber is sporting a short afro and wearing boys clothing.

She told me to make sure I stayed out of trouble, because if I got sent to Juvenile Hall, I would die. She told me about this one girl named Benita who tortured everyone daily. This chick was at least 5'10", 220 pounds, and rolled with a crew of five girls about her size. They would prey on all the new cats by taking their clothes, money, and whatever else they could get their hands on. Amber talked about the day she had a run-in with Benita. Benita put her hands into Amber's pants pockets to take her cigarettes and got her fingers damn near amputated, because Amber kept razors in her pockets to ward off thieves. She told me that so many girls got raped in there it wasn't funny. Sasha, another big girl, tried to rape Amber with a broomstick while she was sleeping. Amber said when she felt the broomstick, she went ballistic on her ass and sliced her fucking stomach wide open. The officials threatened to send her to jail, but it was self-defense, so they left her alone. I would not have been able to survive in a place like that, so I know I am not going to do anything that is going to land me in jail.

I told Amber about my adventures at the theater, and tried to convince her to come with me. I asked her if she ever tried coke and she told me she did, but didn't like the way it made her feel. I didn't agree with her. I loved it because it made me feel invincible. The coke made me feel like I was a sex fiend and the best dick sucker in the world. It allows me to escape. Amber told me that if I continue down the path I'm on, I would end up in Juvenile Hall in no time. She reminded me that if I got caught soliciting people for sex or with drugs in my possession, I would be sent to jail.

She broke my heart when she told me that she could no longer hang out with me because I was a bad influence on her and she needed to focus on getting her life together. Her mother enrolled her into a private school, so we would no longer see each other during the day. I was so upset, and begged her not to leave me. Amber was the only person I cared about. Sonia is living with my father now, and I was looking forward to spending time with Amber. I told her how much I needed her, but my pleas fell on deaf ears. I told her I would stop going to the damn theater and doing drugs just to be with her. She told me I should be ashamed of myself for acting like a whore. I've never been so hurt in my life, and I told her how much I hated her and wished her to hell. I can't believe Amber dumped me. She was the one who introduced me to this lifestyle. How could she just abandon me? I am so glad I met Sue and will be spending more time with her. My mother wants me to visit my father this weekend, but I don't want to visit that bastard and his bitchy girlfriend. I don't understand how Mom can stand to look at him. He treated her like shit for years with his harsh words and adulterous ways.

Signing Off!

December 25, 1987

Dear Diary,

Merry Christmas! I told Sonia my secret about my desire to be with women. I didn't tell her about Amber because I didn't want her to go ballistic. Sonia didn't believe me at first, but told me she loved me no matter what. I didn't know how to tell her about my feelings for boys, too, so I didn't. She asked me if I told Mom, and of course, I didn't. Mom didn't need to know about my sex life. I didn't want her to freak out. I'm confused enough as it is, and didn't want to have to explain myself to my parents yet. I wish Mom would let Sonia come back home because I miss her. Sonia would kill me if she found out about my trips to 42nd Street. I've become accustomed to getting paid for my services, and I'm not ready to stop taking drugs. One of my regular customers pays me three hundred dollars to give him a blow job. Another one of my customers pays Sue and me two hundred dollars to make love to his wife while he watches. I am so doped up most of the time it doesn't matter to me who I have sex with.

Signing off!

January 5, 1988

Dear Diary,

I bumped into Tracy today at the theater and was startled to see her there. I was getting busy with a customer when she walked in with this fine ass white man. She looked at me in disbelief. I begged her not to tell Sonia. She would kill me if she knew what I had been doing. I had always been the rational one and needed to keep it that way. Tracy pulled me aside and told me I needed to stop selling my ass. She asked me how the hell I got into this game. I told her all about Amber and Sue, and she understood. Tracy told me that she occasionally made love to women for money, as well. She asked me if I was ready to become a mother or contract a disease. I told her that if I got pregnant, I would have an abortion. She told me that she got pregnant once and was going to keep the baby, but had a miscarriage in the first trimester. She said that she was doing a lot of drugs at the time and that is why she lost her baby. Tracy shared a lot about her life with me, and I felt sorry for her. That's when I realized for the first time that my life wasn't so bad.

To hear Tracy talk about her mother almost made me cry. Her mother was born in the Dominican Republic and came to the United States for a better life when she was sixteen years old. She moved in with her oldest sister, who was married to a younger man It was only a matter of time before Tracy's mother began sleeping with her sister's husband. When her sister found out, she kicked Tracy's mother out. When the sister's husband found out what happened, he beat his wife down, moved out, and found an apartment for Tracy's mother and him. They lived together for two years, and she ended up giving birth to a son the same day he got deported back to the Dominican Republic. Her mother did not speak English and was unemployed, so she was forced to send her baby to her mother in D.R. It didn't take her long to find another man willing to take care of her, though.

Julius Thomas a.k.a Slick T was a pimp and had a stable of six women. Slick T was a thirty-five-year-old fine ass who loved to beat his women for the hell of it. When he met Tracy's mom, he said it was love at first sight. He wanted to make this woman his wife and his number one whore. Tracy said her mother did not love him, but since he was willing to take care of her, she settled. Slick T didn't know how to love anyone and would sell his own mother's ass if he had to. He introduced Tracy's mom to drugs and despair. She eventually gave birth to Tracy two years later. Tracy said her mother was pregnant three times before he allowed her to give birth to Tracy. He made her abort the other babies. The day Tracy was born, he told her mother as soon as she got home from the hospital he had a client for her. I couldn't believe Tracy's father was so cruel. Tracy's father raped her when she was nine years old and told her he needed to make sure she was ready to begin working. He taught her how to give head and how to shake her ass for the men. She didn't know anything else but to sell her ass. Her main customer was her uncle, her father's brother. Tracy moved in with him when she turned eleven, and he paid a lot of money for her. I felt sorry for Tracy and her mom.

I promised Tracy I would stop. Tracy told me if I didn't, she was going to tell my sister.

Signing off!

January 10, 1988

Dear Diary,

My father convinced Mom to allow him to come over twice a week for dinner. Today was the first one. Sonia convinced me to tell my parents about my preference for women, but I didn't think it was a good idea. Sonia told me that being gay was going to be difficult for me and their support would help me deal with it. After I delivered the shocking news to my parents, my mother looked like she wanted to faint. My father wasted no time cursing me out and said I was an embarrassment to him. I didn't mean to upset Mom because she means the world to me. We were supposed to have a quiet family dinner, and Sonia ruined it. Dad was so pissed off that he left before dinner was served. I have to admit, dinner tasted better without him. I should have told them I was still discovering myself and needed time to work out the various thoughts in my mind.

Sonia is such a selfish wench, and I know she did this to embarrass me in front of my parents. She always wants to be the center of attention. She acts like she knows everything. With all the drama, I needed to smoke a blunt. Since I promised Tracy that I wouldn't go to the theater anymore, I decided to go to Sue's house. When I got there, Sue was so fucked up she had left the door unlocked. Sue didn't hear me enter the room because she was passed out on the couch. I knew where she kept her stash, so I helped myself. I knew she wouldn't mind. While getting high, a beautiful man walked in. His name is Raul, and he is Sue's father. I've seen him there once before, when he gave her money and food. He made me feel uneasy at first, with his bright, blue eyes and hulk-like frame. While Sue was knocked out, we talked and got high together. Before I knew what was happening, we went into Sue's bedroom and made passionate love. This was the first time I made love to someone that kissed every inch of my body. As he kissed me, he gazed into my eyes, and all I could think about was the beach and how calming it made me feel. After what seemed to be hours of lovemaking, we eventually fell asleep in each other's arms. When I finally woke up, he was gone.

I heard moaning as I entered the living room and was shocked to see the man of my dreams on top of Sue, fucking the shit out of her. I was so disgusted *by what I saw going on between them, I almost bolted out of the room. Sue eventually looked up at me embarrassingly and asked me not to leave. Before I knew what overcame me, I began screaming at Raul. She rolled Raul off of her, and they both tried to calm me down. That's when Sue told me he was not her biological father and they've been seeing each other since she was sixteen years old. With Sue now twenty-one years old, that meant they've been together for five years. Raul is thirty-five years old, but looks like he's in his early twenties. I didn't want to get in the middle of their relationship, but this man made me feel good and I wanted to be his woman. On the other hand, Sue was my friend and I didn't want to come between them by sleeping with him. Sue told me Raul was there for her when she needed someone, since her mother was a drug addict and her father was in jail.*

Her father was in jail for molesting her and her little brother. Her father began fondling her when she was five, but never penetrated her or anything. When she told her mother, her mother did not believe her. Her mother finally believed her when she caught her husband trying to force Sue's little brother to suck his dick. They removed Sue's father from the house and sent him to jail. The household finances became nonexistent, and her mother began pros-tituting for money and became addicted to crack. Her mother blamed her children for what happened to them and began abusing them physically. Sue and her brother were sent to foster care for about a year, while their mother went to a rehabilitation center. Sue told me that she tried to kill herself several times that year. Amber told me how crazy the group home was, so I under-stood why Sue wanted to end her life. Sue's mother successfully completed her year at the rehabilitation center and came home with a new husband, Raul. Sue's brother did not want to go back home, so her mother allowed his foster parents to adopt him. Sue was sixteen years old when she moved back home with her mother, and was not happy about having a new father at first. When her mother slipped back into her addiction, Raul made sure Sue had what she needed. Her senior year in high school would have been a disaster if he were not there. On the night of her prom, Raul was the doting father who took pictures and made sure she had a corsage. When she came home from the prom, they made love.

As I listened to Sue go on and on about her love for him, I realized that I did not have a chance with him. I thought their relationship was sick because he was playing the role of her father, and it sounded like he took advantage of her. He was just as disgusting as Tracy's dad in my book. I told Sue about my session with Raul and apologized for sleeping with her man. She assured me they were no longer seeing each other, but slept together once in awhile.

Signing off!

Reading Ashley's journal entry infuriated me and forced me to recall memories I didn't want to remember. Ashley accused me of being self-centered. The only reason I told her to tell our parents was because I thought they would understand. My father should not have responded that way and I was glad when he left, but was not happy about Ashley leaving. Mom was horrified at the news and wanted to talk to Ashley about her feelings, but she didn't get the opportunity to because Ashley ran out of the house. I now know that I gave her bad advice, but I can't do anything about it now. It seems as if Ashley was living a double life. I always thought Ashley was a lesbian and not into men at all. It seems like she had been with plenty. How could Tracy keep this secret from me?

Chapter 6

Ajani and I flew to New Jersey, and he helped me get my father's affairs in order. I'm so glad he came with me, because I would not have been able to handle it by myself. My father lived in East Orange, New Jersey, and boy, has his neighborhood changed for the worse. Papi bought the five-bedroom house for $200,000 four years ago and wanted to sell it for $350,000. Ajani said the house needed a lot of repairs and doubted he would get more than $225,000. Ajani contacted one of his real estate buddies to handle the transaction and fired the realtor my father had hired. Ajani felt the other realtor did not have the experience needed to make this a quick sale. Regardless of what anyone says, Ajani is the man when it comes to handling business.

My father was so happy to see me, and it looked like his depression was instantaneously cured. I decided to remain in my father's house for a few days after he flew to Puerto Rico. Thanksgiving is two weeks away, and I will visit Mom after my trip to California. Ajani couldn't stay with me because he had business to take care of in New York and Miami. I asked him what his plans were for Thanksgiving, and he said he would be going to France as originally planned. Deep down inside, I wanted him to change his mind and spend time with me in Georgia.

I arrived in California on a Sunday, and didn't waste any time creating a schedule for myself. Ajani made sure the house was comfortable and the servants were available to me. I woke up to the smell of fresh flowers and baked bread, making it difficult to leave the house. Santa Barbara is a beautiful city, and I wanted to enjoy every bit of it. So, I made appointments to go wine-tasting on Wednesday and whale watching on Thursday. Although I had to get up early in the morning to visit the winery located on the north side of Santa Barbara, I found the time to read a few more entries from Ashley's journal, which I took along with me. I needed to feel her spirit, and maybe it would help me to finalize my decision.

January 18, 1988

Dear Diary,

Since I caught Sue and Raul in the act, I haven't been to her house in a couple of days, so I decided to stop by after school. When I got there, Sue told me that Raul has been asking about me everyday and really was upset about what happened. Sue told me to watch him carefully and not to trust him. Why should I put faith in her judgment, when she wants him for herself? He came over right when I was getting ready to leave. He apologized to me for sleeping with Sue and me on the same day, and blamed it on the drugs. Raul reminded me of my father in a strange way. I found out he was born in Panama and came to the United States when he was two years old. I asked him to teach me Spanish since my father never bothered to. He said my father should be ashamed of himself for not teaching me. He likes to debate issues, and we discussed the legalization of prostitution and a woman's right to an abortion. I'm against the legalization of prostitution, and I'm for the right to choose abortion if she wants to. Raul strongly opposes abortion, and said he would never allow a woman he was dealing with to abort his baby. Even though he is several years older than me, I felt like an adult.

Signing off!

January 29, 1988

Dear Diary,

Mom and I got into a huge fight yesterday. She received a call from the Attendance Counselor yesterday about my absences from school. I know I was wrong, but I've stopped cutting class. I tried to tell my mother, but she didn't want to hear it. She slapped me across the face so hard that it felt like my jaw was broken. My mother never hit me before, and it startled me. I didn't wait for her to apologize; I had to get away from her, so I went to Sue's house. She wasn't there, but Raul was. I told him what happened and cried uncontrollably in his arms. He told me not to worry, and if I needed a place to stay, I could stay with him and his mother. I took Raul up on his offer and went with him to his home in The Bronx. He lived in a three-bedroom brick house on 233rd Street and Baychester Avenue. When we got there, the house smelled so good from the dinner his mother prepared. It reminded me of the food my abuela used to make when she lived with us. Raul's mother welcomed me into her arms, as if I were her own, and told me to call her Mama Rita. She didn't look old enough to have a son Raul's age. Mama Rita made so much food, it felt like Thanksgiving. The dish I liked the most was the chicken soup they called sancoho. I felt like I found a home, at least until Mom cooled down. Raul was the perfect gentleman. He let me sleep in the spare bedroom and did not try to make any advances toward me. A part of me wanted him to, but I appreciated the respect he showed me.

Signing off!

Chapter 7

The Harrison-Clarke Vineyard & Winery did not disappoint me with their selection of wines. I experienced the taste of Grenache, Cabernet Sauvignon, and the lighter Pinot Noir grapes. My tour guide was very knowledgeable, and I wanted to continue learning more about wine. I thought about Ashley a lot, wishing she was still alive to enjoy the experience with me. I also thought about Ajani and how much I loved being with him. How could I give up this life, the life I've always dreamed about? I was so exhausted that I skipped dinner.

I was glad I scheduled my whale watching excursion when I did, because the Condor Express boat was full. This is the season for the Humpback and Great Blue whales, and there were plenty of whales, dolphins, seals, and sea lions for us to marvel at. We visited the volcanic cliffs of Santa Cruz Island and made a stop at the Painted Cave. My daughter loves whales and would have loved this trip. I felt a twinge of loneliness as I pulled my sweater closer to my skin to keep warm while witnessing a few of the couples and families hugged up with one another. I again thought about how unhappy I am with Ajani and decided to go to a club. After doing a Google search, I went to the nightclub Privilege.

When I got to the club, the crowd was hyped and wild, and it was hard to maneuver to the bar. There were many beautiful women there, and it seemed like hours before someone approached me for a dance.

Martine Alexis was the first man brave enough to ask me to dance. By the time he asked me, I was sulking and nursing my third drink. He is thirty-four years old and lives in San Diego. Martine wasn't as tall as the men I usually date, but he was fine as all hell. He is about 5'9", with olive-colored skin, a bald head, cinnamon brown eyes, and deep dimples in both cheeks. He looked like a little tank, with his bulging muscles and sexy swagger. He kind of reminded me of my boy, Desmond. Desmond's girlfriend, Maritza, killed him three years ago. Maritza was another one of my dead husband's women. Desmond was my sex buddy, and if he were alive, we would still be kicking it. Martine was not as smooth with his line as Desmond, but beggars can't be choosey.

"Hello, Angel. My name is Martine Alexis, and I'm a down-to-earth man. Believe it or not, I came to this club to look for a God-fearing and caring woman."

"It's a pleasure to meet you, Mr. Alexis. My name is Sonia Marlon, and I consider myself a spiritual person," I said.

"As soon as I walked into this place, I noticed you sitting here alone and wondered why. You are an attractive woman, and I feel as if God sent you to me. Let me tell you a little bit about myself. I am easy going, open-minded, and a good listener. I love to laugh a lot, and my friends consider me a comedian. I enjoy going to sporting events and the movies, taking long walks, and dancing. My mother is originally from Ghana, and my father is from Mexico. Now, tell me a little bit about you."

"I'm originally from New York and live in England. We have something in common; my father is Puerto Rican and my mother is African-American. Do you speak Spanish? I don't because my father didn't want us to get confused learning English and Spanish at the same time."

"Yes, I speak Spanish. My father insisted we learn it. He wanted us to have a clear understanding of both our cultures. Are you married or seeing someone?"

"I am seeing someone, but we are going through something right now and need some time apart. What about you? Are you seeing someone?"

"I am dating right now, so I'm not tied down to anyone in particular. My high school sweetheart and I were married for three years before amicably separating. Sometimes I get tired of the dating scene and often think about settling down with the right woman."

"Well, I'm a widow. My husband died three years ago. I love the person I'm with, but he has a difficult time being faithful. I'm not looking to get serious with anyone right now, but I am looking to have a good time."

"Don't give up on love yet. I would love to get to know you and make you smile. As I said when I first approached you, your beauty captivated me. I'm here looking for someone to love and treat me right. Let me treat you like a queen, and I hope you would return the favor and treat me like a king. Sonia, I think I could make you happy, and you wouldn't have to worry about me ever cheating on you."

"Thanks for the compliments, Martine. Why did you and your high school sweetheart separate?"

"My wife wanted to be a medical doctor and felt that I held her back. We argued so much, it wasn't worth it to stay together."

"I do believe you will meet your queen one day, but I don't think you will meet her in the club. Are you a member of a church? That might be a good place for you to look for your soul-mate."

Martine Alexis was too heavy for me and full of shit. His lines are tired and he'll never get a real woman. Once I hit my two dance minimum, I ran to the bathroom for refuge. Upon leaving the restroom, and as I walked through the crowd, someone grabbed my hand. I closed my eyes, hoping that when I turned around there would not be a hot mess standing in front of me. To my delight, there was a smooth chocolate drop standing there with a nice afro and sparkling white teeth. I felt like screaming a loud, "Hallelujah! A man with a dental plan!"

"Hello, beautiful. How are you? My name is Dana Washington, and I live in Benicia, California. I am forty years old and a single parent of an eleven-year-old son. I lost my wife four years ago to lung cancer. I have been lonely for a long time, and right now, I'm searching for true love. This may sound cliché, but I'm here to meet Mrs. Right."

"Wow, this is unbelievable. The first man I met this evening was also looking for Mrs. Right. I'm going to tell you the same thing I told him. I am not here to meet Mr. Right. I just want to have a good time."

"I didn't mean to put you on the spot, but I'm not like the other men in this place who claim to be this or that. I need a woman with dignity, respect, a good sense of humor, and who can be a mother to my son. I know the club might not be the place to meet someone special, but you caught my attention when you walked out of the bathroom and I felt this sudden urge to grab your hand."

"You didn't put me on the spot, and tonight has turned out to be interesting in that I've met two attractive men looking for love. I feel special. I wish you luck on your journey for love."

Damn, cuckoo patrol is out tonight. I went back to the bar and decided to drink until my heart's content. I'm glad I have Ajani, and not out here looking for love in all these dumb faces. Within minutes, a striking White man caught my attention. I stared at him so hard he was forced to look in my direction. After walking over to the bar, he told the bartender he had my drinks for the evening. All I could do was quickly grab an Altoid and pop it in my mouth. He was about 6'4", with ice-blue eyes and a muscular frame. He reminded me of the wrestler from the WWE, John Cena.

"Hello, darling. What's your name? My name is Chris Simon, and I'm a musician. I play the drums."

"Hi, Chris. My name is Sonia Marlon, and thank you for taking care of my tab."

"No problem, Sonia. My rock band has been on tour for two weeks, and after all that performing, I just want to meet some beautiful women and have a good time. I saw you with those other guys and noticed you were not into them."

"Those men were looking for *Mrs. Right*, and I'm not here for that."

"My band has toured all over North America, Europe, China, Japan, and India, and we've recently released a second CD titled The World is

Ours. Why don't you come by and see us perform? We'll be playing at the Roxy tomorrow evening."

"I don't have anything planned, so I'll be there. But, Chris, I would like to continue our conversation in a quieter setting. Why don't we go back to my hotel for an early breakfast?"

"Sure, where are you staying? I'll let my friends know I'm leaving with you."

"I'm staying at the Le Meriden in Beverly Hills, but let's get something straight. We are only having breakfast."

"Great, I'm staying there, too. So, after we eat breakfast, I'll return to my room. I would never take advantage of you."

Mr. Chris Simon was the perfect gentleman and didn't even try to kiss me, but it took everything in my power for me not to pounce on him. I settled for the kiss I placed on his lips, and it was well worth it. Going against my own word, we ended up talking, kissing, and cuddling until five in the morning, and it felt good being in the presence of a man that was into me. During our conversation, I learned that he is not seeing anyone right now and doesn't have any children. I enjoyed his company so much, I didn't want him to leave, but promised to meet him at the Roxy.

✳✳

The next day, I took a trip to Rodeo Drive to get my shop on. Now that I am a size ten, I can wear some of my favorite designers without feeling ashamed. Versace is one of my favorites, so I went to that store first. An attractive Russian guy employed there named Borys helped me with selecting the right outfit for the evening. He quickly discovered what my taste in clothing was and encouraged me to sit down while he went shopping for me. While I waited for him to finish, another store assistant brought me champagne to drink. Borys did a superb job in finding me an outfit for the evening, along with other clothing. In fact, I bought more clothing than I intended on. After leaving Versace, I tried to enter The House of Bijan, but was told I had to make an appointment. Like the tourist I was, I peered into the boutique and marveled at the colored crystal chandeliers hanging from the ceiling. Another spectator told me the chandeliers were made from over one thousand authentic Bijan perfume bottles. I also noticed the names of his clients permanently engraved on the front window. Tracy would have made a fool out of us by demanding entry into the store if she were here.

When I arrived at the Roxy that evening, I felt a little overdressed, but was determined to enjoy myself even though I am not into rock music. Three other bands performed before Chris and his band went on. In my opinion, Chris' band outperformed everyone. After their performance, Chris and I had dinner at the Rainbow Bar & Grill, which is located next door to the Roxy. We shared a plate of spicy Buffalo wings and a large pepperoni pizza pie.

Wanting to show my appreciation, I let Chris take me back to his hotel room, where we made love. He was not the best I've ever had, but I enjoyed him anyway. Unfortunately, I had to slip out like a thief in the night because I had a flight to catch to Georgia in the morning. Before leaving, though, I left my cell phone number and e-mail address on his pillow.

Chapter 8

Mom was happy I finally decided to visit her, but was annoyed with me for not bringing Ashley. Don't get me wrong, I love my daughter, but it's hard for me to look at her and not see Mark. I lost my sister and my friend Desmond because of him, and it's hard for me to get past it. I think that's why Ajani adopted Jasmine, because he knew I was having a difficult time getting close to her. It's better for her that I stay out of her life, because I know I wouldn't treat her right.

Mom took me to some impressive and stately neighborhoods in an attempt to get me to move to Georgia. One of the communities we went to is called Sandstone Estates located in Lithonia, Georgia. The homes were massive, but not what I'm accustomed to living in. Mom lives in Alpharetta, so it took us over an hour to get to her house. Atlanta's traffic is one of the reasons I would not want to move to Georgia. It takes too long to get anywhere.

Tracy called while I was getting ready for bed. She wants to come to England in December. I told her that she should come to Georgia and spend some time with Mom, and then we could fly to England together. In a way, I'm glad she declined the offer because Mom does not like Tracy, and I didn't feel like hearing her mouth. Ajani also called and was annoyingly pleasant.

"Hello, darling. How is your mother doing? Tell her I'm sorry for not spending Thanksgiving with her, but tell her Christmas is at our house. How was California? I hope you behaved yourself."

"Ajani, I had a wonderful time in California. It's too bad you were not able to join me."

"I'm glad to hear you enjoyed yourself. Maybe we can visit together in July. Did you get an opportunity to go wine tasting?"

"I went wine-tasting *and* whale-watching. I also went to Rodeo Drive for a little shopping. Tracy called just before you did and said she wants to come to England in December. She did not give me an exact date, though. I hope you don't mind."

"No problem. It will be good to see her again. Charles will make the arrangements for her to fly on my private jet."

"Did you close the deal in Miami?"

"No, I didn't close the deal on the nightclub because they have not completed the renovations outlined in the contract. The weather in St. Tropez has been horrible, so you made the right decision to visit your mother. You would not have been happy. I love you, Sonia. I'll see you in a couple of weeks."

I never thought I would fall in love with someone again, but Ajani has managed to get me to do just that. However, after meeting and spending time with Chris, I began to question the love I have for Ajani. I've come to the realization that money is not going to keep me happy. I went through a lot with Mark, and I didn't want to jump into anything serious until I got my head together. Ajani's perception of our relationship is different from mine, though, and I know I cannot trust him to be faithful to me.

Will I ever find out the truth about his relationship with Chelsea? I doubt it. Even though he told me he is no longer seeing her, deep down inside I know he is lying. Chelsea means much more to him than the other women he's had affairs with. Alike's words still ring in my head. *Ajani is too powerful for you! You don't know how to handle a man of his caliber.* When I think about her words, I can't believe I've stooped so low in an attempt to prove her wrong. I decided to give her a call to see how she is doing and to congratulate her on her engagement. She would give me the full scoop on Chelsea.

"I am so glad you called, Sonia. I haven't spoken to you in a long time. How are you and your family doing? I'm truly sorry about what happened to your sister. I'm such a horrible friend. I should have kept in touch with you, but I've been dealing with my own demons."

"Alike, I've been extremely upset with you since Ashley's murder. When I needed you the most, you treated me shitty. Do you remember when I called you to help get me a flight out of New York and you ignored me? And why didn't you attend Ashley's funeral? I thought you were a friend, Alike. It has taken me three years to forgive you. So what demons are you battling now?"

I don't know where all of this anger came from. My goal was not to bombard Alike with all of those questions.

"I am sorry, Sonia, about the way I behaved, but I was doing some heavy drugs during that time and couldn't even keep my own shit together. I've been riding a rollercoaster all my life, and it finally jumped the tracks on my ass. When Mom died, it only got worst. I don't know if you've ever spoken to Charles before, but he is more than a driver. He is Ajani's confidant and my friend. Charles sat me down one day and told me that I had to get help for my addiction. He found a six-month drug rehabilitation program in Arizona, and I checked in immediately. The program helped me uncover the pain I felt when I was raped. When I successfully completed the program, I went back to New York. I was clean for two months before I started using again. Charles was still there for me, and this time, he found a program that had inpatient and outpatient services. I stayed at the facility for three months, and I am still participating in their outpatient program. I've been drug free for six months now, and I feel so much better. I met my fiancé David during one of the group counseling sessions. He has been drug free for three years. We dated for four months before getting engaged last month. We're going to get married in August of this year instead of June, and I hope you will be able to attend."

"I'm sorry to hear about your mother's passing. Please accept my condolences. I am ecstatic to hear about your new love life, though. Tell me more about this lucky man. It's so good you have found love."

"David Adamson is an attorney and originally from Boston. He's Caucasian and ten years younger than I am. He has two teenage daughters who live with their mother. I don't believe I ever told you about my son, Jao, who is seventeen years old and lives with his father in North Carolina. When you meet David, I know you will like him. We are not living together and have opted not to engage in sexual intercourse until we wed. I know that might sound strange to you, but I realized that anything worth having is worth waiting for. I've hired a wedding planner to make sure my wedding is like the fairytales I have read about in books. I plan on arriving to the wedding in a horse-drawn carriage."

"Alike, I'm so happy for you. I can't wait to meet your son. I'm sure he is as handsome as you are beautiful. How did his father get custody of him?"

"My ex-husband left me when Jao was two years old, and got custody of him when he was eight. He had good reasons for leaving me and taking our son with him. I was so far gone. I tried to raise Jao on my own for those six years, but the drugs and fast life called and I followed. The straw that broke the camel's back was when I went out of town for the weekend and left Jao home alone. At the time, I thought he would be alright because I left enough food and water for him. Jao was smart enough to call his father to come and get him. I didn't fight for custody because I was wrong for leaving him home alone."

"I'm so sorry to hear about your troubles, but am glad you are better now. Ajani asked me to marry him, and I told him no. He is not accepting no for an answer, though, and told me to take some time to think about it. Do you remember telling me that I couldn't handle, Ajani? You told me that Tracy was a better woman for him. That statement has haunted me for years.

"You did the right thing by not accepting his proposal. Ajani is a selfish bastard, and you could do much better. I apologize for hurting you, Sonia, but I stand by what I said. Tracy knows how to deal with a man like Ajani. She would never fall head over heels in love with anyone for the sake of love. She would accept his money and enjoy life."

"You're right because he has never been faithful to me. I was under the impression that we've been seeing each other exclusively, but he recently told me that was not the case. He doesn't deserve a woman of my caliber. I need a man that can commit to me. But the real purpose of my call is to get some information about Chelsea. I'm fully aware of their relationship, so don't worry about my feelings."

"You've put me on the spot, Sonia. I don't even know where to begin. However, it's interesting that Ajani proposed to you, since he is already engaged to Chelsea. They are having a baby in June and have set the wedding date for April. My only hope is that the demon child she is carrying doesn't kill her during childbirth like his first wife."

"Why did he propose to me if he is already engaged? He told me that they are no longer seeing each other. None of this shit makes sense to me. I'm not African and will not go into a polygamist relationship with him. You mentioned that Ajani was married in the past, but I don't believe you. He never said anything to me about being married."

I had to pretend like I didn't know because Tracy shared this information with me in confidence.

"I don't know what to tell you, Sonia. I have seen him with her several times. They've had dinner with my fiancé and me on several occasions. She went with him to Miami and St. Tropez for the holidays. It's up to you whether you believe me or not. You knew what kind of man you were dealing with. I'm sure you're sorry you didn't let Tracy take care of him," she said with a chuckle.

"I should have let Tracy *keep* him. I was attracted to his money, and I must admit that I am no better than Tracy. When Tracy first met him, I was jealous of her catch and wanted him for myself. Now, I consider this another lesson in life."

"There is a price to pay for beauty, they say. Are you willing to sell your soul for it? I know what it feels like to be in love with Ajani. It took me a long time to get over him, and to be honest, it takes everything in my power to stay away from Ajani because he brings up bad memories for me. He introduced me to drugs and the fast life. When we met, I was working with a legitimate modeling agency and not using drugs at the time. He didn't get addicted to drugs, but when I did, he started treating me differently. Has he told you about us or his affiliation to my escort business?"

"Did he give you the money to start the business, Alike?"

"Hell, he owns it. I'm just the front-person for the business. He supplies all the customers and I provide the women."

"Thanks for the info! I always enjoy talking to you, Alike. I wish you much success with your marriage, and don't forget to send me an invitation. I will call you in a couple of months to give you my new address. Ciao."

"Wait, Sonia. I can be so abrasive at times. I'm sorry. You asked me about Chelsea, and I didn't want to lie to you. But it's about time you knew what your man was doing behind your back. I'm a changed woman and here for you if you need me. Sonia, it's time for you to move on and out of his home. If you want to come back to New York, I can help you find an apartment. If you need to stay with me, let me know."

"I don't know what I'm going to do yet, but I'm certain that I will not be returning to New York. Ajani adopted Jasmine, so I will leave her with him."

"Yes, Ajani would give you a hard time if you tried to take her away from him. Hey, let's think about this for a minute. You could always call his bluff and accept his hand in marriage. See what he does. What could it hurt? You could marry him before she does. Marriage is like a business, and Ajani has a lot of money for you to play with. Love is an important factor…I know, because I love David…but consider your options. You're a smart woman. Why don't you visit me in New York for a weekend to get your mind off of him? We can go shopping and go to a Broadway play or something."

"I am so tired of playing games with Mr. Ajani. Why should I marry him just to prevent someone else from being with him? Hell no! She can have the fucker."

"Sonia, think like Ajani for a minute. Why do you think he got involved with Chelsea? She probably has something he wants or needs. He only thinks about himself. Even if you don't believe this now, I know he loves you, but he doesn't know what to do. Chelsea is accepted by his friends and fits into his image. I say call his bluff and marry him. Think of this as a business deal. You have nothing to lose."

"I have everything to lose, like my self-respect and dignity. I do not have to compete for his affection, and I am not willing to share him with another woman or stand in the way of him having a relationship with his child."

"What in the hell does love have to do with anything? Tell me! You loved Mark, and how did that help you? Think about it, seriously. I'm sorry to have upset you, Sonia. Whatever you do, don't tell Ajani I said anything to you."

"Thanks, Alike, but there is not much to think about. My mind is made up, and I've decided to leave him. I appreciate you for telling me the truth and will not tell Ajani you told me."

"Look, I have an awesome idea and business opportunity for you. You love to cook and do it so well, right? Why don't you cater my wedding?"

"As much as I love to cook, I'm not interested in the catering business, so I must decline. I will see you at the wedding, though. I'll be in Georgia for one more week, and then I'm heading back to England to get my belongings together. I forgot to tell you that Tracy will be visiting us in December. So, I will leave England for good after she departs."

"Sonia, if I were you, I wouldn't trust Tracy around my man. I know you guys have been friends for years, but I'm telling you to break all ties with her because she doesn't have your best interest at heart."

"Why would you say that? Didn't you offer her a place to stay, too? Tracy has her moments, but she has always held it down for me when I needed her to. She was almost killed because she was protecting me."

I knew I couldn't trust Tracy, but I wanted Alike to tell me why.

"Forget I said anything. I don't want to come between you and your friend. My only concern is for your sanity. I think she still has feelings for Ajani, and I'm pretty sure she will try to take Ajani away from you. Ajani was always smitten with her. And yes, I did offer her a place to stay until she found somewhere else to live, but don't think you can't stay with me, too. Let me know what you decide to do about Ajani."

"Thanks again for the offer, Alike, but I will not need to stay with you. The house in Santa Barbara is in my name, so I will live there for awhile. Ajani is already engaged, and as I mentioned earlier, I will not stand in his way."

That heifer is crazy if she thinks I'm going to marry that trifling man. What I *will* do is get out of the way so Chelsea can have him. Mom and I are going to Buckhead, Atlanta to meet a few of her friends for lunch, and I'm not looking forward to it. In an attempt to lift my spirits, I decided to give Chris a call before we left. It's only been a few days since I snuck out of his room. I hope he isn't mad at me.

"Hi, Chris. This is Sonia. I'm sorry about sneaking out of your room, but I had a plane to catch. I hope you can forgive me. How was your Thanksgiving?"

"Hello, Mystery Lady. I didn't think I would ever hear from you again. Thanksgiving was good and soulful. I've fallen in love with collard greens and sweet potato pie."

"Now that I know you like collards and sweet potato pie, I'm going to have to make some for you. I'll be in Georgia for another week. It's too bad we can't see each other again before I go back home."

"I would love to see you again, too, but my schedule will not permit it. I'll be touring for the next six months. Our final stop is Detroit, and then, I have to head right back to Canada for the Montreal Jazz Festival in June. If you haven't been to the festival, you would enjoy it. You could stay with me if you decide to come."

"Sounds like a plan, but I thought you lived in Toronto. You just said the festival is in Montreal. Explain to me how that would work."

"Okay, you busted me. I'm inviting you to stay in Canada with me for a couple of weeks. I'm staying at the Hilton in Montreal. You can stay with me until the festival is over, and then, we'll go to Toronto together."

"It's too bad I can't see you before June. My calendar is free and I would love to meet you in Detroit."

"Touring is grueling, and sometimes I can get a tad bit grouchy. I wouldn't want to expose you to that side of me."

"Alright, I won't be pushy with you. I'll be patient and wait until June. In the meantime, let's remain in contact with each other."

Chapter 9

It's the middle of December, and we have been experiencing some bad weather in England these last couple of days. I guess being in California and Georgia spoiled me with the nice weather.

Tracy arrived today, and when that diva got off the plane, I was sorry I asked her to come. She looked like she put on a few extra pounds and had a boob job. I felt like someone kicked me in the stomach. She wore the hell out of the Rocawear sweat suit, and she made a statement with that outfit that I heard loud and clear. She's rocking a Spanish wavy weave that looks like it grew right out of her scalp. Ajani could not control his gaze, as his eyes remained fixated on her ass. I didn't want to cause a scene, so I kept my composure by not slapping the taste out of his mouth. Alike told me to be careful, and I chose to ignore her once again. I will keep a close eye on these bastards, though. Overall, it was good to see my friend, and I hope my fears are for nothing.

"Tracy, you look good. I'm so happy you finally made it. How long are you staying?" I asked, secretly wishing her visit would be a short one.

"Thanks for sending your plane for me, Ajani. I've never flown on a private jet before, and I want to compliment your staff on their service. They made certain my champagne glass stayed filled and I had enough to eat. Sonia, you're a lucky woman to have a man that can fly you around the world in his private jet," she said coyly.

"I'm glad you enjoyed your flight. We were a little worried you would not be arriving on time because of the horrible weather," he said.

"To answer your question, Sonia, I'll be here for two weeks or longer. Alike's condo will be ready for me in three weeks. She asked me to be her maid of honor, so I need to find a dress that shows off my new curves. In addition, I have a baby shower to go to next month."

"Has Alike decided on her colors yet? She told me that she wants to have a storybook wedding, so I'm assuming white is going to be one of the colors. While we are shopping, I need to make sure I get something, too."

"I believe Alike is going to dress in a traditional African wedding gown, with the primary colors being chocolate, rust, and cream. I'm looking for a rust-colored ensemble."

"Who's having a baby?" I inquired.

"A very good friend of mine named Chelsea is having her baby in June. She's also getting married in March or April, I think," Tracy replied.

If looks could kill, Tracy would have been dead already. Ajani looked like he wanted to wring Tracy's neck and dump her body in the river. I was not going to let Tracy know what I knew, though.

"Tracy, Charles will take you anywhere you need to go," Ajani said. "I'm so happy for Alike and David. They make such a nice couple. I don't know if Sonia told anyone yet, but I proposed to her before Thanksgiving. I hope she will say yes, so we can begin planning for our wedding."

"Really? Sonia, you should have told me Ajani proposed to you. Are you keeping secrets from your friend?"

"I haven't told anyone about Ajani's proposal. I need more time to think about it."

"Ajani, you know my friend Chelsea? Did she send you a wedding invitation? I know she would love for you to come to her wedding."

"Sonia and I will attend Alike's wedding in August. Tracy, please excuse Sonia and I," Ajani interrupted.

"Ajani, would this be the same Chelsea you've been seeing? I heard she was pregnant and was due any day now," I said.

Tracy had this look of victory on her face that I wanted to slap off.

"Sonia, let me talk to you for a minute in private. I do not want to discuss our personal business in front of Tracy. Let's go to our bedroom."

"No problem, darling. Tracy, I would love for you to make yourself at home. The room you will be sleeping in is next to the servant's quarters."

"I hope I haven't started any trouble. I just wanted to update you guys on the social events in New York. I would have preferred to sleep in one of the rooms upstairs on the third floor, but I guess they are unavailable. Good night all, and to all a good night."

"You are correct, Tracy. The room is no longer available. Your room has been refreshed, and I think you will be real comfortable there," I stated firmly.

That whore sauntered off like I was supposed to feel sorry for her ass. She is lucky I didn't put her stank tail back on the plane.
Ajani grabbed me by the arm and led me to the bedroom.

"Sonia, I didn't want you to find out this way. I didn't know how to tell you that Chelsea was expecting my baby. I asked her to marry me because I felt it was the right thing to do since she was pregnant. I fucked up, and I am sorry. I feel as if I'm always apologizing to you."

"No problem, Ajani. You told me that you and I were not seeing each other exclusively, so it doesn't matter. You were right in asking her to marry you, and I wish you all the best. Did she enjoy the villa in St. Tropez? You didn't have to lie to me about breaking up with her. I'm a big girl. I can handle it."

"I'm not going to ask how you obtained that information, but I will ask for you to forgive me."

"Forgive you for what? You didn't do anything to me."

"Sonia, I'm going to call the wedding off with Chelsea. I do not want to marry her. Please accept my hand in marriage, Sonia. I want *you* to be my wife and be a part of my child's life."

"Stop lying to me for once in your life. You've been playing me for a fool, and I no longer want to be with you. I now know the reason you didn't want me to go with you to Miami; it's because you were spending time with Chelsea. There is no reason to continue with the lies. I will not marry you, and have decided to move to California once Tracy leaves. I do have one question for you, though. When were you going to tell me about the baby?"

"I didn't know how to tell you, and probably would have told you after Tracy left. Don't leave me, Sonia. We can work it out. We've invested three years of our lives together; let's not give up so easily."

"Whatever, Ajani. You are so full of shit. Thank you for all the good times, but it's time for us to move on. You will always have a place in my heart. I wish you and Chelsea all the best. When will Chelsea be moving to Europe?"

"She is not moving to England because I am not going to marry her. I need to talk to my attorney about getting joint custody of my baby."

"Ajani, you no longer need to convince me about your decision to marry or not marry Chelsea. Whatever you decide to do is your business."

Ajani is a master at fucking people's heads up, and I had allowed him to play with my emotions, for too long. How in the hell did he think he could get away with this shit? That bastard is going to pay for what he has done! Alike is right; it is time to plan my wedding.

Chapter 10

After I went to bed and thought about what this motherfucker was doing to me, I decided to fuck with *his* head. So, I slipped into his bedroom and put it on him. A part of me wanted to walk away from him, but the competitive side of me wanted to fight for my man. Chelsea knew about me, and still, she continued seeing Ajani because she thought I was not good enough for him. Well, she was going to learn what it meant to fuck with me.

Ajani is a weak man and a sucker for some good loving. So, I made sure to wake him and make passionate love to him. He woke up to warmed jasmine-laced oil all over his body. I watched his facial expressions as the oil touched his skin; he couldn't control himself. I straddled him, and as he entered me slowly, I looked into his honey-colored eyes and thought about how much I wanted him to pay for making me love his stanking ass. I looked into his eyes once more and then proceeded to give him what I knew he wanted. I didn't want him to think he didn't mean the world to me, so I showed him how much he meant to me with each stroke. That bastard thought it was going to be easy. Oh, the hell it was. Chelsea had a fight on her hands.

We made love for what seemed to be hours. I fell asleep afterwards, and when I woke up, I smelled the sweet scent of fresh roses and the aroma of hazelnut coffee. Ajani made sure to have Anissa put fresh roses in the room. When I went downstairs to the kitchen, there was banana bread, Belgian waffles with whipped cream on top, and a glass of freshly squeezed orange juice waiting for me. As I drank the orange juice, I noticed a pink diamond ring at the bottom of the champagne glass. It was breathtaking, and I almost passed out when he dropped to one knee and asked me to marry him while placing the ring on my finger. It took all I had not to kick him in the fucking face. He thought I was an idiot.

"Sonia, you are the love of my life. I love you so much that I don't mind getting on my knees and begging you to accept me as your husband. I know it has been difficult these last few years, and I want to make it up to you by giving you the world. I have done you wrong so many times and I'm sorry. Let me be the man I know I can be. I am asking you again to be my wife."

"Ajani, I don't know what to say. I don't know if I can accept this ring."

I could only hear Alike's voice in my ear, saying, "You stupid bitch, marry his ass."

"We can get through this. I know we can."

"Ajani, you have been there for me in ways I'll never be able to repay you, and I appreciate all you've done for me. I just want to make the right decision this time. When Mark and I married, it felt right... perfect...but look how it turned out. I don't want to go through that same experience again."

"I understand, Sonia, but I'm a much better man than Mark was. I know I have a long way to go to prove my love to you, but give me a chance and I'll show you. I've only loved one other woman, and she died during childbirth. You can't imagine the pain I endured since I lost her. It has been so difficult to love someone like that again. With Chelsea being pregnant, I felt that God was giving me a second chance at love, but I realize now that you are the one I love."

"I am sorry to hear about your loss. I know what it feels like to lose someone you love. Marriage is serious business, and before I marry again, I need to make sure it is right. Give me some time to think about it. I'll let you know soon."

I already knew I would marry him. I've learned my lesson, and I know a leopard cannot change his spots. All I care about is my future, and if I can get some money out of the deal, then I will be alright. Alike is right. What in the hell does love have to do with it?

I haven't read Ashley's diary in awhile, so I'm compelled to sneak a peak into it again. Reading her diary might give me the answers I'm looking for.

January 31, 1988

Dear Diary,

I ran into Sonia at school today, and she told me Mom was sorry about what happened and was worried sick about me. Sonia suggested I go home and talk to Mom. I told her I wasn't ready yet, but to tell Mom I was okay. Sonia has a lot of nerve. She knows how Mom is and that is why she is living with Pops.

Raul and I were determined to keep our relationship a secret from Mama Rita, because she would not approve nor condone him sleeping with a minor. I didn't know how long I would be allowed to live with them before my mother would call the cops. Mama Rita told me I was always welcome to stay with them, but needed to talk to my mother. I was happy she allowed me into their home, but I knew she was right because my mother would call the police on her.

When I called Mom, she apologized for the way things transpired between us. She asked me if I wanted to come home and I told her no. It broke my heart to hear her sniffling over the phone. I needed time to think and wasn't ready to go home. Mama Rita spoke to Mom and told her it was okay for me to stay with them until I was ready to go home. I was surprised my mother agreed.

Signing off!

March 12, 1988,

Dear Diary,

I missed my period last month, and I didn't think anything of it initially. But when I threw up, I had a feeling I was pregnant. I went to the clinic yesterday, and they told me I was two months pregnant. I was alarmed, scared, and happy at the same time. When I told Raul, he was so excited and asked me to marry him. Since I'm only fifteen, I knew I needed to get permission from my mother. Raul had it all figured out; his ex-girlfriend works at the Marriage License office, and would hook us up. I was so excited I told him yes, but we had to tell Mama Rita. I didn't want to break Mama Rita's heart, but I think she would be happy about having a grandchild. As soon as we told Mama Rita, she began to scream at me. She told me I shamed their house and made a liar out of her. She was responsible for me and I disappointed her by sleeping with her son. She threatened to call the cops on Raul for sleeping with a minor and to send me back to my mother. I didn't want to go back home. Mama Rita and my mother decided it would be best for me to have an abortion and move back in with my mother. She told my mother about her experience working with troubled girls and that it was important I lived in a stable and healthy environment.

Mama Rita wanted to talk to me alone, so we went to dinner. She wanted to make sure my relationship with her son was consensual and that he did not rape me. She did not approve of us getting married and would not allow it. She told me that Raul was a troubled man and that he would not be a good husband or father. She knew he sold drugs and about Sue, and doubted they ever stopped seeing each other. I didn't know what to do. I've never had to make these kinds of decisions before. I told her I did not want to go back home pregnant nor did I want to have an abortion. She agreed to allow me to stay with her until the baby was born in October. Since we only had a few months before school let out, I figured I could finish school without anyone noticing I was pregnant.

Mama Rita is such a wonderful person and offered to get me a job in her office. We are still going through with our wedding plans and are going ring shopping in a few days.

Signing off!

March 25, 1988

Dear Diary,

I went to Sue's apartment today to tell her the good news and was surprised by what she told me. Raul married her three days ago and she was three months pregnant with their second child. I was surprised to hear about her being pregnant with their second child when I didn't even know about the first one. She told me about their two-year-old son Raul Jr. who is in foster care. He was taken away from her because she left him at school. I couldn't believe my ears. How could they do this to me? She told me Raul never intended on getting me pregnant or marrying me. They lied about the seriousness of their relationship. I should have known better, but I was so naïve and stupid. I've been deceived. I am beginning to think I should listen to Mama Rita and have an abortion.

I needed to talk to someone, so I gave Tracy a call out of the blue. When I told her about the situation, she told me to give the baby up for adoption and go back home. I didn't want to give my baby up, but I knew I was in no position to take care of a child on my own. I really messed up big time, trying to be all grown.

Signing off!

I am ashamed to admit I did not have the faintest idea of what was going on with my sister. I recall her running away from home, but didn't know my mother approved of this arrangement. If my father didn't act like an asshole, Ashley could have lived with us instead of strangers. Mom had a lot of explaining to do about why she let Ashley live with a complete stranger. Now that I think about it, Mom had a new boyfriend and probably didn't want to be bothered with her children. You have to really wonder what was going on in her mind. She never told me or my father about Ashley's pregnancy. I decided to call my mother and tell her what I read. I hope she tells me the truth. I believe if my father knew what was really going on, he would have allowed Ashley to stay with us; at least I hope he would have.

Chapter 11

"Mom, how are you doing? I have good and bad news for you. Which do you want to hear first?" I asked.

"Sonia, I am too old to play games with you. Tell me what you want me to know."

"Ashley had a baby when she was a teenager. I've been reading her diary, and I'm up to the part where she writes about being pregnant."

"Do you know for sure she had the baby? She might have had a miscarriage. Don't call me with all of these speculations. Finish reading the damn diary, girl."

"I have a strong feeling Ashley delivered. I am certain. What are we going to do about it, Mom? We have to find our flesh and blood."

"What if Ashley had an abortion? She could not take care of herself, much less a baby. She didn't have much of a choice anyway, because I was going to have Raul arrested if she kept the baby."

"How could you be so cruel, Mother? It was Ashley's right as a human being to decide and not yours."

"Ashley had her whole life ahead of her, and she shouldn't have to sacrifice her life for children."

"Is that what you did when you had us? I hoped a small piece of Ashley's life was still left here on this earth, and you just took it away from me. Since you seem to have all the answers, I have one question for you. Why did you allow her to live with a stranger?"

"Sonia, I don't feel I have to explain anything to you. I tried my best with you girls. It was very hard for me as a single mom. Everything I tried to do, you all challenged me on it. I got tired of fighting you all at some point. You lived with your father and he was a stranger, so what's your point? Why should I take the emotional beating? I did the best for the both of you, and you both wanted to act like assholes. So, I literally gave up. Do you remember all the times you threatened to go live with your father when I enforced the rules of not staying out late? I didn't want you to live with your father. I didn't want him to know I lost control; I didn't want to seem as if I was a failure. I failed at marriage and at motherhood. Ashley wanted to live with Rita, so I let her. I was miserable with and without you girls. I was so happy when she finally came back home, though."

"Mom, did Ashley have an abortion or not? You have not given me a straight answer yet. And why did you give up so easily? We needed you to be strong for us."

"I did not give up on you all; I just needed a break. Where is your daughter? Where was she when you and Mark were having problems? How could you be so judgmental of me? I suggest you take a close look in the mirror at yourself."

"Why are you getting so defensive? Jasmine is in boarding school, where she is getting an excellent education."

"Jasmine was carted off to boarding school as if she was a nuisance. She could have gone to a private school and still live at home with you. Do you see Mark in her? Maybe that's it. You are ashamed of what her father turned into and now you want to banish her from your life. I told you that Mark was no good. His mother was a convicted felon and drug addict. Where was his father? I wanted so much more for you, but you wanted to marry him. Don't blame your daughter for your decisions. Her father is dead, and now her mother doesn't want her."

"Mom, you are cruel! I love Jasmine and so does Ajani. She has not been banished to boarding school. She has many friends and enjoys being there. Don't try to transfer your guilt to me."

"Jasmine should be at home with you. I know you are grown, but

I'm your mother and my opinion still counts. You said that I gave up on you and your sister. Well, what do you think you are doing to your own daughter? Don't make the same mistakes I made."

"You are entitled to your opinion, but Jasmine is going to remain in boarding school for now. What I want to know is how could Ashley keep such a secret from me? I confided in her about what was going on with me, but I guess she didn't feel she could do the same. I am especially disappointed in Tracy because she was supposed to be my road dog. How could she have kept this secret from me, too? By the way, she is visiting Ajani and me for a couple of weeks."

"You know I never really liked Tracy. I tolerated her because I felt sorry for her, with her mother being strung out on drugs. The girl grew up on the street, so what does she know about loyalty? My advice to you is to keep her close and away from your man."

"Mom, knowing she held this secret from me, I don't trust her at all. In addition, I spoke to Alike, and she shared some disturbing news about Ajani. She also told me Tracy knew about them, as well. I'm going to suggest she cuts her vacation short with us. Ajani and I need to talk about a few things."

"You've been warned. I don't know what else to say on that subject. I have many errands to run, so I'll talk to you later."

I was glad Mom abruptly got off the phone because she was starting to annoy me. She is a hypocrite and a liar. I was hoping she would tell me if Ashley had the baby or the abortion, but she stuck to her guns. She didn't even apologize for her mistakes. No wonder I'm cracked up in the head. Who can I trust, if I can't even trust my own mother?

Let's hope the answers to my questions are in Ashley's journal. If she had the baby, I'm sure she would have written about it.

March 27, 1988

Dear Diary,

After finding out about Raul and Sue, my decision was made to have the abortion and go back home and concentrate on me. I felt compelled to focus on getting my grades up so I can apply to college. Mama Rita and I had a long talk about my decision, and she offered to go with me. I told Mama Rita about Raul and Sue, and I apologized for taking advantage of her kindness. She was very upset to hear about Raul Jr. and is going to find out how she can obtain custody of him. She told me Raul came home late last night and was acting strange. When she asked what was going on, he told her he was moving out. We both knew he went to go live with Sue. As I think back on the last few months, I can't believe I got myself in this mess. Mama Rita told me my life was not over and that God was giving me a second chance to follow my dreams. Her words were so comforting, and I shared my thoughts of becoming a lawyer with her. She told me to go for it.

Signing off!

March 29, 1988

Dear Diary,

I went to the library today to do some research and saw my ex-girlfriend, Amber. She looked like an entirely different person from when we last saw each other. She no longer looked like a butch, and I almost didn't recognize her. Amber always kept her hair short and in a punk rock style; now she had a shoulder-length weave and was wearing a fitted turquoise sweater dress with high-heeled black boots. When she noticed me staring at her, she looked right through me as if we never met. I was hurt by her actions and tried to act like it didn't bother me, but it did. Amber was with a very nice looking, brown-skinned, tall, African-American young man. I knew she was trying to make me jealous by kissing and hugging her friend, and I was. How did I allow this girl to hurt me? When she went to the restroom, I followed her, determined to get my two cents in.

As soon as she walked out of the stall, I began to tell her off. She put her hand in my face and told me to back off. I was so angry I wanted to smash her face into the mirror, but I kept my composure. She asked me what I wanted, and I told her that I wanted to know why she cut me off. She told me that I was a bad influence and headed down a path she just came from. After I calmed down, we talked like civilized people. I was happy to hear about her passing the GED and her acceptance into college. She will be attending the University of Alaska in the fall. She gave her life to Christ and was thankful for the many blessings she received. My family was not into the church nor did we have discussions about God. Mama Rita was Catholic and went to church from time to time, but we never discussed God. It was kind of weird hearing about God and Jesus Christ for the first time from my friend. I noticed the glow in her face as she spoke about what God did for her, and I wanted to experience the same feeling.

When I told her I was pregnant, she immediately gave me a hug and told me everything would be okay. I tried to hold back the tears, but they flowed uncontrollably down my face. Amber held me close and told me God represented love and would forgive me if I asked him for forgiveness. I was a little unsure of what she was talking about, but it sounded hopeful. She invited me to her church, and I promised to visit. When I told her I was considering having an abortion, she asked why I would kill a human being when all I had to do was give the baby up for adoption. She suggested I talk to her mother who works for the Department of Social Services. Her mother could help me get public assistance and or refer me to an adoption agency if I decided not to keep the baby. I told her my mind was made up. I didn't want anyone else to raise my child, so having an abortion would be better for me.

I didn't know how I went from being a straight "A" student to a pregnant fifteen-year-old. Talking to Amber gave me hope. If she could change her life around, so could I. It seems like it was only yesterday I was home with my mother, eating her famous apple pie and playing spades with Sonia. The thought of me being a teen mom never crossed my mind. I'm not ready to become a mother right now, and when the time is right, I want to be able to give my child or children everything they could possibly need without struggling.

Amber apologized for taking advantage of me. I told her I never felt like she took advantage of me, but was really hurt when she left me. I really loved our friendship and enjoyed the short time we spent together. She told me she still likes women, but since it is a sin, her pastor is counseling her. The pastor used to be gay, and his life changed when he went to a church that counseled *gay people. The counseling sessions were intense, and it took him ten years to rid himself of the demon of homosexuality. He is now married with five children. I wished her luck, but didn't believe a person could change their sexual preference. I believe her pastor is suppressing his true feelings, and in time, he will go back to being with men, if he isn't already seeing them on the side. I couldn't say I enjoyed being with one or the other, women or men. I enjoyed the relationship I had with her and Raul. It was good seeing Amber, but I couldn't help but feel a little lonely for Raul. I wanted to be in a loving relationship with someone.*

Signing off!

April 3, 1988

Dear Diary,

Tracy and I had a long conversation yesterday. She was very happy when I told her that I was going to have an abortion, and she even offered to go with me. I'm scheduled to have the procedure done in two days, and I'm a little scared of what might happen to me. Mom agreed to go with me, as well, so I'll have a lot of support.

Signing off!

April 11, 1998

Dear Diary,

I lost my baby six days ago. Raul showed up at the house the day I was getting ready to go to the abortion clinic. I don't know how Raul found out, but he knew, and told me that he would not allow me to abort his baby. When I told him he had no right to tell me what to do, he slapped me in the mouth. I punched him in the face, and he slammed me against the wall and continued to punch me repeatedly in the face and chest. It felt like I was going to die.

When Mama Rita came home, she found me balled up on the floor holding my stomach, while Raul kicked me in the face. She hit him over the head with a lamp to make him stop. She rushed me to the hospital and I lost my baby. The attack left me with a broken jaw, cracked collarbone, and a broken arm. The doctor told me that I was lucky to be alive. Mama Rita called the police and told them where to find Raul. They arrested him at Sue's house. He was the second person in my short dating life to break my heart. Is this what love is all about? I don't want to love another person. Every time I fall in love, I get hurt. He took advantage of me and hurt me in a way I'll never forget.

Signing off!

May 19, 1988

Dear Diary,

After the attack, I was hospitalized for eight days. The Department of Child Welfare got involved and wanted to place me into foster care, but Mom knew someone and I was allowed to go back home with her. We started seeing a family therapist a few weeks ago. The therapist's name is Dr. Angeles, and I really like her. My life feels like it's in shambles, even though everyone keeps telling me I have a bright future and that all I went through will make me stronger.

Mama Rita calls me everyday to see how I am doing. She told me that he was charged with statutory rape of a minor, assault, and a few other charges, and will probably have to do some jail time. I asked her if he said anything about me, and she said he was sorry for hurting me and causing me to lose the baby. He told her when he found out I was going to abort the baby, he just lost control, and didn't mean to hurt me. Mama Rita told me Raul has been abusing drugs for years and was high on crack that day. Out of concern for Sue and the child she was carrying, Mama Rita convinced Sue to move in with her until the baby was born. She also hired a lawyer to gain custody of Raul Jr.

Signing off!

Reading Ashley's diary drains me, but I feel closer to my sister than ever before. I still can't believe Mom knew about all this, yet kept it a secret from my father and me.

Chapter 12

I woke up this morning feeling like a brand new woman. Reading Ashley's journal confirms in my mind that I am truly alone. If I marry Ajani, I can at least live life through my dreams. He has the money to make all of my dreams and wishes come true. Alike is right...marriage *is* a business. Since I made him beg, I think the best way to accept his proposal would be to tell him yes in front of his closest friends. If they think I'm not good enough for him, it's time they find out who the real Sonia Marlon is. I'm going to arrange a party announcing our engagement and get Alike to help me. There is something about Alike I really admire. We've gone through a lot over the years, but she has always kept it real with me.

While sitting on the bed thinking about my great idea, something compelled me to look out the window, and to my amazement, I saw Ajani and Tracy in a love-locked embrace. They were naked and consumed with themselves. How could they disrespect me in my own house? I wanted to run downstairs and blow their heads off, but decided against it. Instead, I ran to the closet and took out my camcorder to videotape them in action.

I made up my mind; Tracy and I would no longer be friends. The love I had for Ajani went out the window with each stroke I witnessed. I'm so pissed off right now and don't know what to do. A part of me wants to go on with my idea to marry him so I can make his life a living hell, but the rational side of me knows marrying him would be a big mistake. My former husband put me through this same nonsense, but this time, I'm going to be rewarded for my discomfort.

I continued taping as they made love without a care in the world. I thought about the advice my sister would give me, and that would be to get the hell out of town. Whereas, Alike would tell me to consider this a business deal and secure my future.

I needed a plan and a strong drink. I drew myself a bubble bath and poured a tall glass of Vodka on the rocks. After soaking long in my bubble bath, I called Alike to tell her what I witnessed.

"I told you not to trust that skank. I'm so glad you videotaped their stupid butts, but I still want you to go through with marrying him. Tracy thinks she is slick and has a hold over him. What she doesn't realize is she's just a trick. She is so jealous of your relationship. I wouldn't be surprised if they've been sleeping together all along."

"That bitch doesn't care about anyone but herself. How dare she come into my house and disrespect me? I've always been there for her, and this is how she treats me? I really want to kick some ass right now. I will not be able to play it off for long without confronting them. Maybe I'll invite them to the theater room downstairs to watch my homemade movie. I hate them so much. Ajani doesn't know who he's messing with. He thinks I'm going to continue to sit back and allow him to trample over me. Well, I have news for his ass; I have someone on the side, too. The writing is on the wall; it's time for me to leave him."

"Sonia, don't be stupid. Are you going to let Tracy come into your home and take your man? You need to stay right where you are. *You* are the woman of the house."

"Can you believe before I caught them in the act, I was thinking of having an engagement party?"

"I will help you with the party. When were you thinking of having it? Chelsea's baby shower is in January, so maybe we could have your engagement party the week before her shower. I will invite all of his friends, except for Chelsea. I want her to hear the good news through the grapevine. Hey, I have an even better idea! Why don't you two get married the day of her baby shower? Think about where you would like to get married so I can have David get your marriage license."

"Alike, I am not going to marry Ajani. Tracy can have him. I'm going to call my secret lover to see if I can hook up with him this weekend."

"Sonia, trust me, my plan will work. Now tell me where you would like to exchange nuptial vows. The South of France would be marvelous, but expensive. You could also have it at your home, which would be even better. Let me know what you want to do."

"I have to admit your idea is ingenious. But, I am still going to see my friend. I'm supposed to be visiting him in Montreal in June."

"Okay, you don't have to give him up, but you have to be careful. I love you, Sonia. Things will work out. Trust me on this one. I know you love Ajani and it hurts every time he does something like this, but he is a man. You have to admit one thing, he asked you to marry him, something I was never able to get him to do. I know what I'm saying sounds ludicrous, but I know he loves you."

"It doesn't make sense to me. If you love someone, why would you do everything in your power to hurt them?"

"I don't know what to tell you. Men are like that sometimes when they are afraid of giving their heart and soul to one person. It takes a lot for people in general to share their innermost thoughts and desires with one person. I am sure you will see a change in him once you wed. Let's not forget Tracy's role in this. You know she seduced him. He *is* a man, and it can be hard for them to say no to a beautiful woman."

"Ajani is a grown man. He should have left the pool as soon as she started coming on to him. I think he still has feelings for her. He was so happy when I told him she wanted to visit us. Tracy is a fucking tramp, and I want her out of my house now. I'm going to confront them, Alike. How am I going to look at myself in the mirror knowing the bitch slept with my man and I didn't say anything? It's bad enough I have to deal with Chelsea and didn't think I had to compete for his affection with my best friend."

"Don't say a word to them. Let Ajani tell you what happened. If he truly loves you, he will. Think about it, Sonia. I'll call you in a couple of days."

As I entered the kitchen, I thought about grabbing a knife, but the smell of hazelnut coffee and freshly baked bread and cinnamon buns calmed my nerves. Carmella is the best cook/baker around, and we are fortunate to have her working for us. I asked her to make a lavish breakfast consisting of a vegetable omelet, biscuits, bacon, and sausage for Tracy and Ajani while I went shopping for a wedding gown. I've always admired Vera Wang gowns, and hope I can find one in my size since I don't have time to get it altered.

While shopping, Ajani blew up my phone, but I refused to answer. Why was he so concerned about my whereabouts now? Maybe he feels guilty about what he did this morning. Oh well, it's not my problem.

I purposely hired a private driver to take me around so Ajani wouldn't know where I was going. I found a small boutique located in London that had an assortment of elegant wedding gowns. I selected a satin dress in gold, which was laced with Swarovski crystals. The cathedral-length train sealed the deal. The dress looked good on me, but still needed to be altered a little. However, the owner of the store promised the dress would be ready in a couple of weeks.

When I returned home, Tracy and Ajani were having cocktails in the study. Ajani jumped up and greeted me with a kiss. I had on very dark shades, so he couldn't see the disgust in my eyes.

"Sonia, I was so worried about you. Where were you? Did you get my message? I've left several of them on your phone."

"I went to London to do a little shopping. I neglected to charge my phone last night, and it died after I spoke to Alike. How was your day? I hope breakfast was satisfying?" I said with a smirk on my face.

"Carmella made a wonderful breakfast. I only wish you were home to enjoy it with us."

"You know I'm trying to maintain my figure, so I only had some coffee and fruit this morning. It was important for me to make sure my best friend had a hearty breakfast, though, since she is only visiting us for a short time. Tracy, did you enjoy the cinnamon buns with the orange and cream cheese icing? They are my favorite."

"The breakfast was delicious and very fattening. The cinnamon buns were the best I've ever tasted. Why didn't you wait for me? Didn't I tell you I had to go shopping for Alike's wedding?"

"I didn't want to disturb your sleep after such a long flight yesterday. By the way, I found a very elegant dress to wear to Alike's wedding. I called Alike to find out the colors of her wedding, and she said her theme is French inspired."

"Maybe you could show me your dress after we finish drinking our cocktails. Why don't you join us?" Tracy insisted.

"Why didn't you tell Charles to take you this morning instead of hiring a private driver?" Ajani interrupted. "Charles would have taken you with no problem. Matter of fact, he had a few errands to run for me downtown. It doesn't make sense to pay an outside company when we have a very capable driver," he stated.

"I hate disturbing Charles with my last-minute plans. If you folks don't mind, I'm going to pass on having drinks and retire to bed early. I have a very busy day tomorrow."

"Did you eat already? Carmella made your favorite Brazilian dishes: crab shells stuffed with crabmeat, shrimp stew, kale, and doce de leite pastry with caramel. Would you like me to make a plate for you?"

"How kind of you, Ajani. You are always the perfect gentleman, but no thank you. I'll have some for lunch tomorrow," I replied with a smirk.

"I'll join you then, Sonia. Good night, Tracy," Ajani said.

"You are not being a good host, Ajani. You should stay up with Tracy," I said with a laugh.

"Tracy will be fine without me. I have an extremely busy day tomorrow, so I need some rest. I hope you don't mind, Tracy."

"It was great talking to you, Ajani, but don't stay up on my account. Sonia, let's go shopping tomorrow. I want to spend some time with my friend."

"No problem. I'll have Miranda wake you up after my swim. I usually swim five laps a day, but I didn't wake up in enough time to do it this morning. So, that means I have to swim ten laps tomorrow."

If looks could kill, I would have been dead. Ajani and Tracy's expressions were priceless. I didn't want to show my hand, but I couldn't resist making a wise comment regarding the pool. I really wished Ajani would continue entertaining Tracy, but he wouldn't have it.

Chapter 13

"Good afternoon, darling. How is my beautiful bride-to-be?"

"Good afternoon, Ajani. I'm wonderful. What time are you planning to go to London?"

"I took the day off so I could spend it with you and Tracy. I noticed you didn't get up this morning to go swimming. What happened?"

"I overslept again. I guess I was more tired than I thought."

"You most definitely overslept, because it's two o'clock in the afternoon. So I guess you will swim fifteen laps tomorrow," Ajani chuckled.

"Charles went ahead and took Tracy shopping. I hope you don't mind. Why don't you come downstairs and have breakfast with me? Carmella made your favorite."

"Oh, okay. I have one quick question for you first, Ajani, and I hope you can answer it."

"I'll answer all of your questions, but I also want you to answer my question."

"I don't know if I can your question right now, Ajani. Give me a couple more days. I promise I will answer your question no later than Saturday. Ajani, can you be faithful to me? I want you to really consider your answer. The institution of marriage is very important me. I was a schoolgirl in love when I first got married, but this time is different because I'm older. In order for me to accept your proposal, you must respect and commit to me. If you don't think you can remain faithful to me, then you've answered your own question. Chelsea is carrying your child, so there will always be a connection between the two of you, but I will not marry you if you cannot remain faithful."

"Sonia, I love you very much. Once we are married, I promise to be faithful."

"As I said before, you don't have to answer my question right now. I want you to really think about your response."

"I don't need to think about my feelings for you. As I said, once we are married, I will remain faithful to you. Hey, we haven't gone out in a long time, and I would love to go to the Royal Opera House to see *Il Trovatore* and have dinner at one of your favorite restaurants."

"What about Tracy? I feel bad about not spending time with her."

"She will be fine, and you know she'll have Charles take her everywhere she wants to go. You know how she loves to shop."

When we went downstairs, I marveled at the display of floral arrangements in the kitchen and really felt loved. If I were a few years younger, I would have told Ajani right then and there, "Yes, I will marry you and all is forgiven." However, I know this man will never be faithful to me; he is only trying to play me for a fool. He is so persistent about marrying me all of a sudden, and it makes me wonder what his motive is. I guess we will soon find out what he is up to at the engagement party.

While Ajani was on the phone handling some business, I decided to read more of Ashley's journal.

May 25, 1988

Dear Diary,

Mom and I see Dr. Angeles every other week to discuss some of my issues. Dr. Angeles always sees me first, then she talks to Mom alone, and then we talk as a group. Dr. Angeles is an excellent therapist and really knows how to get me to open up and share my feelings. Mom has been great since I came back home, but you can tell we have some unfinished business to deal with.

One of the reasons we don't get along is because Mom refuses to listen and always has to be right. Mom refuses to hear my side of the story and insists I was the cause of all my problems. I agree to some extent that I am stubborn, but when I needed her, she gave up on me, just like she did to Sonia. She complains about how Sonia and I were miserable children and didn't have respect for her. I felt she should have stood up for me when my father degraded me with his cruel words. I really didn't want to hear her excuses.

These sessions force me to remember the things I've been trying to forget. She asked a lot of questions about my early years and about the relationship I have with my parents. I told her about the way my father treated my mother. I never felt connected to him, and Dr. Angeles wanted to know why. She asked a lot of questions about my father's family and if he's ever taken us to Puerto Rico to visit his family. I told her he was ashamed of them and his mother didn't like my mother. She asked me how I felt about my grandmother and I told her I loved her because she was family, but I didn't really know her. When she visited us, she always antagonized Mom and there was a fight. Mom would yell at Dad for allowing his mother to disrespect her. Dad is macho and would hit Mom when he felt she got out of line. Mom said his mother was prejudice and didn't deserve to have such precious grandchildren. I remember Grandma being mean to Sonia. Sonia would cry every day until Grandma left. Grandma would always look at Sonia and say to her "cabeza del nappy" or "nappy head". Grandma didn't treat me bad, and would always bring me a doll from Puerto Rico. Mom said that she preferred me over Sonia because I was light-skinned and my eyes were hazel-colored.

While reminiscing about my father's family, I recalled the first time we met my father's little brother, Uncle Saul. I was six, Sonia was nine, and he was fifteen. Sonia and I were mesmerized with his good looks and had a crush on him. Uncle Saul was gorgeous with his cocoa-colored eyes and jet black, curly hair. He spoke more English than his mother, and at first, was fun to be around. Grandma sent Uncle Saul to live with us because he was getting into a lot of trouble in Puerto Rico and needed a male role model. When we first met, he said I was his favorite, and Sonia was jealous of the attention he gave me. He called me "mi pequeña muchacha especial" or "my little special girl". Dr. Angeles pressed on about Uncle Saul. When I found myself crying uncontrol-

lably, she had to stop the session. I didn't want to talk anymore about Uncle
Saul ever again. He did things to me I am so ashamed of.

Mom held me in her arms and told me how much she loved me. I felt her
tears as she cradled me in her arms. I know she wanted to know what he did
to me, but I wasn't ready to talk about it. She didn't do her job as a mother.
She was supposed to protect me, and she didn't.

Signing off!

May 30, 1988

Dear Diary,

Ever since I had the breakdown in Dr. Angeles' office, Mom has been ex-
tremely nice to me. I decided to tell her what Uncle Saul did, and I can tell
she wanted to kill somebody. Mom told me what Saul did to me was unaccept-
able and not my fault. She asked me if Sonia knew what was going on and
if he bothered her, too. Uncle Saul told me if I agreed to let him fuck me, he
wouldn't bother Sonia. Mom was so angry that she called my father and told
him what happened. He called me a liar. From that point on, my father was
dead to me. I hated everything about him and his crazy-ass family. Mom told
me things would get better now. I do feel better, and for the first time in a long
time, I have hope.

Signing off!

I remember Uncle Saul and how much I hated him. He promised me
if I let him stick his dick inside me and did what he wanted, he would
leave Ashley alone. That sleazy motherfucker broke his promise. I never
told anyone about Uncle Saul, not even Mark. Uncle Saul lived with us
for three years, and those were the worst three years of my life.

Chapter 14

"Good morning, Sonia. How was your evening last night? I hear you and Ajani are horrible hosts."

"What do you mean? Have you been speaking to Tracy?"

"Why, of course. That stank bitch called me last night before she went dancing. Is she home yet?"

"Don't know where she is. I'm still in bed. Ajani and I went to the Royal Opera House last night and had a wonderful time."

"Sonia, she admitted to sleeping with Ajani and expressed her hatred for you. Do you know why Tracy hates you so much?"

"She has no reason to hate me. I've done nothing to her. She is the one keeping secrets from me. I've been nothing but honest with her."

"She blames you for taking Ajani away from her, even though she chose to be with Sheila."

"Is she still using drugs? She doesn't appear to be rational."

"Tracy was never a rational person, and I don't know about her drug habit. The only thing I know for sure is she despises you. Hey, I will be leaving New York tomorrow to go to Paris to meet with the designer and could make a pit stop in London for a few days, if you would like me to," Alike said.

"Sounds like a great idea. Do you want to stay with us?"

"No, I'll stay at The Ritz. I don't want Tracy or Ajani to know I will be in town. Tracy is a dangerous woman and should be handled by someone like me. Do you still want to have the surprise engagement party? I only have a few weeks to plan. Would you like to use my wedding planner? She is pricey, but you can afford it," she laughed.

"He is really trying to make amends. The big issue for me is he slept with my best friend and doesn't seem remorseful. As much as I want Chelsea and Tracy to suffer and envy me, I will be the one stuck with him. I'm not sure I want to go through with this."

"Sonia, don't change your mind. It's too late anyway."

"What do you mean it's too late? It's not like anyone else knows about this."

"I forgot to tell you I sent out a thousand invitations to your surprise engagement party. We don't have much time, Sonia. I'm sorry I neglected to tell you about it."

"I want to be with him forever, Alike. I guess you knew what was in my heart."

"Well then, we will continue on as planned without regrets."

"What if he decides not go through with this? I don't want to be embarrassed."

"Stop playing games and claim your man."

"Okay, Alike, I'll go through with it. I would like the wedding to take place in our lovely rose garden. How many people do you think will actually show up?"

"We can expect at least seven hundred people to show up. Where would you like to go for your honeymoon?"

"St. Martin. I found a villa in Terres Basses, St. Martin that we can rent out for one week. You should think about going there for your honeymoon."

"St. Martin is beautiful. I did a fashion show there when I was younger. Is the villa near the water?"

"The villa overlooks the Bay and has a cascading pool, six bedrooms, and seven bathrooms. If we like the place, I'm going to persuade him to sell the villa in St. Tropez, since he ruined it for me by taking Chelsea there."

"We are going to take a cruise for our honeymoon so we can island hop."

"That sounds like a good idea, too, but I'd rather go to St. Martin. It will give us the alone time we need. Since you seem to have everything under control, here's the number so you can make the arrangements... 1-800-555-6712."

"It will all be taken care of. Don't worry. When I arrive, we'll go shopping for wedding bands. I haven't selected ours yet, and it'll be fun. Talk to you soon."

As I was deep in thought, Tracy entered my room looking frustrated and bent out of shape.

"What's up, Sonia? I feel as if you are ignoring me. We haven't spent anytime together, and I want to know why."

"What is your problem? I'm sorry if you feel that way. You will be here for a while, so we have plenty of time to hang out. How was the club last night?"

"You've been ignoring me, but it's okay. The club was definitely off the chain. I danced the whole night. You should have been there with me. You have become such a damn prude."

"Tracy, I've just had a lot on my mind lately. Ajani proposed to me, knowing full well that's what I want most in the world."

"Are you really considering marrying him? The man is already engaged to someone else. Chelsea is sporting a big belly *and* a rock on her finger. Don't be foolish and think for one minute he is going to marry you."

"He doesn't love her, and he only proposed to her because she is pregnant."

"Who told you that lie? Chelsea is known and loved by Ajani's friends. You are the one they don't like. Everyone knows the only reason you are still in England is because he feels sorry for you."

"Really? Is that what everyone thinks? They think I'm a charity case? What about you? Do you think I'm a charity case, too? Is that why you decided to visit me after all this time?"

"You are not a charity case, but you can be so naïve at times. How long did you think this fairytale would last, Sonia? I'm here for you, just like I've always been. I don't want you to continue making a fool of yourself."

"Well, it seems as if I'm a fool in more ways than one."

"What do you mean by that? I hope you are not referring to me. I've always looked out for you, Sonia."

"Why are you being so defensive? I was not referring to you."

"I didn't appreciate your tone. Do what you want to do. You'll never learn, and I can't help you anymore."

"Thanks for all of your help, Tracy. I'm so lucky to have a friend like you, who is always taking care of me *and* my man. By the way, when will you be leaving?"

"I meant to tell you I am cutting my vacation short. Alike said my room will be ready next week, so I will be leaving on Sunday. I hope you don't mind."

"No problem. We have four more days together, So let's make sure the next couple of days are well spent. I don't want you to return home without seeing some of the beautiful sites England has to offer."

"That would be nice. We haven't seen each other in awhile, and I was looking forward to spending some time with you."

"Have you ever gone horseback riding? I would like to make arrangements for us to go to the countryside on Saturday morning. We can go dancing on Friday."

"I've never gone horseback riding before and would love to go. Is Ajani joining us?"

"Yes, but why are you so concerned with his affairs? You seem to really be concerned about Ajani's whereabouts. Do you still have feelings for him?"

Tracy chuckled. "I was just wondering, Sonia. I no longer have feelings for Mr. Ajani, and am appalled you would even imply such a thing. You know, if I didn't decide to stay with Sheila, Ajani would have been my man. And if he was my man, Chelsea would not be pregnant. I know how to keep a man like him satisfied."

"You really think Ajani would have stayed with you for three years? I don't think so, Tracy. He likes a woman with class, and you are not a class act. If his friends don't like me, they sure as hell would not approve of you. He would be ashamed to take you around his friends and business associates. He wouldn't want his friends to know his woman was a recovering addict or prostitute."

"He wouldn't have to take me around his friends. I would be his secret lover. Right now, you're concerned about his late night meetings. Well, that wouldn't be a concern for me because he would be coming home every night on time to be with me. But, Sonia, don't worry; I am not after your man. You and Chelsea can continue to fight over his cheating ass."

As she walked away, all I could think about was bashing her in the head with my fist. This bitch thinks I am so stupid. I was hoping she would at least admit to sleeping with Ajani. She is such a hoe, and I can't wait to see her face when Ajani and I say, "I Do".

Chapter 15

It is three in the morning, and today is the day of the engagement party. I feel as though I'm about to hyperventilate. It seems like it was only yesterday when Alike came to town and helped me pick out our wedding bands at Harry Winston. I tried to keep the engagement party a secret from Ajani, but it was hard. I can still see Ajani's face when I told him I would marry him. Tears streamed down his face as he kissed my hands profusely. He was excited about the engagement party and suggested we make it official in May.

Alike was instrumental in making sure the wedding planner did everything right. I feel guilty for not inviting my mother, but I'm still upset with her.

"Good morning, Ajani. How is my loving husband-to-be doing?"

"I am the happiest man alive. I still can't believe you agreed to be my wife. Come to think of it, I never asked you what changed your mind and would like to know."

"It was a hard decision for me, but I took the time to really think about what you meant to me. I thought really hard about what it would be like without you in my life, and it felt really barren. You have done a lot to hurt me, but you've also given me joy. I could not have handled Ashley's death without you by my side."

"Sonia, I have something to tell you about Tracy, and there's a lot I have to share with you before we get married."

"I would appreciate your honesty. Do I need to sit down for this?"

"No, you do not need to sit down. As I've said several times, you are a beautiful woman, and I'm sorry it took so long for me to realize that. Thank you for deciding to marry me, and I promise I will do everything in my power to make up for all of the pain. I am not happy about what I'm about to tell you, but I promised you that I would be truthful. Tracy and I made love in our swimming pool when she was visiting us. I don't have feelings for Tracy, but she would not take no for an answer. I tried to avoid her advances, but when she went down on me, I lost it. I told her I didn't want to, but my little friend down below wouldn't cooperate. You don't know how guilty I feel about what happened.

"Also, I have another confession about Chelsea. Chelsea's uncle is a longtime business associate of mine, and that's how we met. She came to England ten years ago to attend an award ceremony. We dated for five years before ending our relationship the night I met Tracy. My feelings for Tracy were purely animalistic. I remember the first time I laid eyes on Tracy at the Waldorf Astoria; it was lust at first sight. I ignored Chelsea the entire night as I preyed on Tracy. Chelsea is very laid back and watched me pursue Tracy, but said nothing. We shared an apartment together in Manhattan, and when I got home, she was gone. We rekindled our relationship last year after we ran into each other in New York.

"Chelsea and I made a good team, or at least that's what everyone said. Chelsea's parents loved me and wanted us to get married. Her father is a judge in North Carolina and we often played golf together. Chelsea had everything growing up, so she didn't need my money, which was a problem for me. Sometimes I want to introduce my lady to something new, and I couldn't do that with her.

"Sonia, you didn't come from a privileged background, so when I take you someplace you've never been before, you appreciate it. You remind me of my first wife. She was a poor, young woman from Belize. Her parents had twelve children, and she was their youngest daughter. I gave them ten thousand dollars for her hand in marriage. I was twenty-five years old at the time, and she was fourteen. Her name was

Antolina, and she died during childbirth."

"I'm so sorry for your loss, and I thank you for being honest with me, Ajani. I have a question about Antolina, and I hope you don't take it the wrong way. How could you marry a child? Antolina was too young to be a mother."

"She was not considered young. Most women in her village were married at the age of nine. My mother married my father when she was fourteen, so it was not strange or unacceptable to me."

"Did you tell Chelsea about us? Does she know you will not be attending the baby shower today?"

"I have not been honest with her, either. I told her that I would not be able to make the baby shower because I had a very important meeting that could not be postponed."

"Tell her tomorrow; she deserves to know the truth. And what about the baby?"

"She knows I will be a responsible father, but let's not ruin our day talking about Chelsea."

"I knew you would tell me the truth, and that's the reason I agreed to marry you."

Ajani finally told me the truth, and I consider this a sign from God that he is ready for marriage.

❊❊

"Sonia, you are going to make a beautiful bride. Where is Ajani?"

"Thanks, Alike. Ajani is taking a shower. I told him to hurry up and put his tuxedo on and meet us by the rose garden. How many people showed up?"

"About six hundred of his pompous ass friends are here, and they don't have a clue this engagement party is for you. They will be surprised to see you instead of Chelsea. In the meantime, they are enjoying the hor d'oeuvres of crab stuffed lobster tails, petite filet mignons with jumbo lump crab cakes, a tray of smoked salmon, clams, and mussels, and Alaskan crab legs. The main course will be served as soon as you and Ajani arrive. Carmella prepared Portuguese cuisine for the occasion, and it will include grilled Norwegian salmon with Port wine and raisin sauce, grilled filet mignon with Cabernet sauce and wild mushrooms, seared loin pork with littleneck clams, and pan-roasted chicken with mashed potatoes. The guests will go home with a bottle of Perrier-Jouet Brut Fleur de Champagne."

"You are so funny, Alike. I thought you included my name on the invites. At least they're eating well. Let's hope no one chokes on their food when they realize they've been duped."

"They would not be here if your name was on those invitations. I'm sorry to tell you this, but Ajani's friends really like Chelsea."

"They are so full of shit. I never liked them anyway. What about, Tracy?"

"I didn't invite her ass. I didn't think you would want her to attend."

✧✧

As Ajani and I drove toward the rose garden, I noticed the white lights alongside the walkway. The rose garden was transformed into a Winter Wonderland, and I felt like Alice. When I stepped out of the limousine, white doves were released into the sky as Jeffrey Osborne's "On the Wings of Love" played.

I thought it was strange that my father was there to greet me. *What is going on?* As I looked into Ajani's eyes and immediately realized that today was our wedding day, I started to cry. I was glad to be marrying the man of dreams. I couldn't stop the flood of tears falling down my freshly made-up face. As my father and I walked down the aisle, I noticed my mother crying and her boyfriend Teddi smiling from ear to ear. I wanted to kill Alike for keeping this from me, but at the same time, thank her for making this the best day ever. I felt like I was having an out-of-body experience as I listened to the preacher.

"Friends, we have been invited here today to share with Ajani and Sonia a very important moment in their lives. In the years they have been together, their love and understanding of each other has grown and matured, and now they have decided to live their lives together as husband and wife. Ajani would like to read a poem he wrote."

"Sonia, your favorite flowers are roses, so I chose a poem demonstrating my love for you.

The red rose silently sings the love I have for you,
While the white rose exhales, each warm breath I take seeps through my heart,
The red rose is a symbol of my love that lurks around you everyday,
And the white rose is a dove flying amidst the clouds.
But I bring to you a cream-colored rose with highlights of pink,
Indicating the pureness of our love and trueness of our friendship.
Everyday I have desires of our oneness to be forever true,
Longing for both of our lips to subtly touch.

"I, Ajani, take you, Sonia, to be my partner. Loving what I know of you, and trusting what I do not yet know. I eagerly anticipate the chance for us to grow together, getting to know the woman you will become, and falling in love with you a little more each day. I promise to love and cherish you through whatever life may bring us."

"Since I didn't know today was going to be my wedding day, I did not come prepared, so I will repeat your words to me. Ajani, I take you to be my partner. Loving what I know of you, and trusting what I do not yet know. I eagerly anticipate the chance for us to grow together, getting to know the man you will become, and falling in love with you a little more each day. I promise to love and cherish you through whatever life may bring us."

Then the pastor said those heavenly words..."By the power vested in me, I now pronounce you husband and wife. You may now kiss the bride. I now present to you Mr. and Mrs. Omaro."

Chapter 16

Two months later.

"Good Morning, Sonia. How are the newlyweds doing?"

"Mom, everything is great! How are you doing? I'm still floating on cloud nine right now. Alike made all my dreams come true."

"Have you heard from Tracy lately? She did not look too happy on your wedding day. She had Charles take her to the airport immediately after you and Ajani left for your honeymoon."

"Tracy and I had an argument just before she left, and was convinced Ajani would not marry me. What she didn't know is we really love each other. Mom, I must admit, I've been very upset with you, too."

"Sonia, what did I do to upset you?"

"Mom, you kept secrets from me. I'm your daughter, too, but after reading Ashley's journal, I feel as if you loved her more. Why didn't you tell me what was going on with my sister?"

"Ashley did not want you or your father to know. It was not my place to include you."

"So you both conspired against me. Why was I the only one in the dark? Ashley confided in Tracy, when *I* was her flesh and blood."

"The relationship you had with your sister was between you guys. You have to take a look at yourself. Did you do everything you could to make your relationship work when you were younger?"

"Ashley should have come to me. I was the first person she told about being a lesbian. I looked to Ashley for advice, and I assumed she looked at me in the same way. Tracy hurt me, too, by not telling me what was going on with my sister. We were supposed to be best friends."

"You know how I feel about her, but that has nothing to do with you. If the relationship between the two of you is over, then let it go and move on. A lot went on, Sonia, right before your eyes, and you didn't notice it because you were consumed with what was going on with you. You and your father got along so well because you both are selfish people. You think the world revolves around you. Did you know how much Tracy suffered in high school? Ashley did, because they talked a lot when you were hanging out with Mark and his family."

"Tracy revealed to me a couple of years ago about her life. Reading Ashley's journal enlightened me on how close Tracy and Ashley were, but I'm not going to beat myself up about something I can't change. The past is the past!"

"There is another secret I'm keeping for your sister, and I guess it's time I tell you."

"What is it now? Was Ashley sleeping with Mark, too? Or better yet, Tracy was her girlfriend."

"No, Ashley got pregnant again during her last year at Hampton."

"Who was the father, and did she keep the baby?"

"She had twin girls, and the father was Raul. He blamed her for his imprisonment and tracked her down like a dog. Ashley had an off-campus apartment and often came home late. One night, she came home and Raul was in her apartment waiting for her. He told her that he was truly sorry for what he did and wanted to rekindle their relationship. She responded by saying she was not interested in dating anyone at the time because school was a priority. He didn't like her answer, so he raped and beat her repeatedly throughout the night. He told her that he was going to make sure she had his baby and would kill her if she didn't keep it."

"So this motherfucker threatened her life again? Why didn't she call the police?"

"She did call the cops, and he was arrested. She did not find out she was pregnant until she was in her sixth month when she missed her period. When she graduated, she was seven months pregnant, and eight months when the babies were born. I'll never forget that beautiful day...June 23, 1994. Mama Rita and I were there when those beautiful babies were born. Ashley loved those girls and I know she wanted to keep them, but she also wanted to pursue her dream of becoming a lawyer. Rita offered to take care of the babies until she graduated from law school."

"Mom, Ashley never made it to law school. So what happened to the babies?"

"Ashley got a job offer in New York as a paralegal and didn't want to pass up the opportunity. Rita took the children to Florida where she had a home."

"Where are my nieces now? What are their names?"

"I haven't heard from them since Ashley was killed. Briana and Bria should be about eleven years old."

"Who choose their names? And have you seen them? If so, when did you see them last?"

"Ashley named them, and yes, I've seen them. The last time I saw them was when they were three years old. Rita invited me to spend the holidays with them. Ashley did not go with me because she was openly gay at the time and didn't want Rita to know.

"Was Ashley ashamed about being a lesbian? I thought she was comfortable with it."

"She *was* comfortable with her sexuality, but she wasn't ready to share that part of her life with Rita."

"Didn't Ashley want to see her children? How could she abandon them?"

"She didn't want to be pregnant. She despised their father, and thought the best person to take care of them was Rita. She wanted to forget that part of her life, and asked me to never discuss the girls with her again. Rita was good about sending pictures to me and Ashley, but Ashley never opened the envelopes. Deep down inside, she loved her children, but she couldn't handle the pressure and responsibilities of motherhood."

"I guess Ashley and I had a lot in common, because I'm dealing with the same feelings about my own daughter. When I see Jasmine, I see Mark, and that is difficult for me. I want to erase everything about him from my mind. Ajani is an excellent father and loves her very much. Even though Jasmine is in boarding school, Ajani is very involved in her day-to-day schedule. He spends a lot of time working with her teachers to make sure she is getting what she needs academically and socially. I don't want my daughter to grow up thinking her mother doesn't love her. Bria and Brianna are the same age as Ashley, and I think it is time they meet one another. What do they look like? Please send me their pictures, and give me Ms. Rita's information so I can contact her."

"Rita was honest with them from the beginning, and told them all about their parents. After your sister died, Samantha sent me an envelope with a letter Ashley wrote to her girls. I sent the letter to Rita along with pictures of Ashley, and she will give it to the girls when they get older."

"Wasn't Raul married to Ashley's friend, Sue? What happened to her?"

"After Sue found out about the rape, she divorced him, married a man in the military, and had two more children. The children she had with Raul remained with Rita. It's been three years since I last spoke to Rita. One of her friends told me that she has a new husband and they live in North Carolina. Rita has her hands full, so I'm glad she found someone to help her with those children. I offered to keep them over the summer when they were younger, but she said they were involved in many activities. Brianna is a ballerina and Bria is a violinist."

"I want to meet them. They need to know they have an auntie who loves them. I remember reading about Raul Jr. in Ashley's journal. How old is he now?"

"Raul Jr. graduated from high school and is on his way to boot camp. I'll see if I can get more information on their whereabouts."

"Mom, you should have told me before. I had a right to know I had nieces. Do they know about me or Daddy?"

"Ashley did not talk about you or your father with Rita. Ashley chose Rita to raise those babies as her own, and it is Rita's decision to tell those girls about Ashley's other family members. Ashley did not want your father to know anything about her, and you know that. How could you even mention his name? You know how much Ashley hated your father. As I said earlier, I'll do what I can to locate them and let you know what I find out."

"There should be no secrets between family members. I don't agree with you or Ms. Rita, but I thank you for sharing this information with me today."

"I respected your sister's wishes by keeping this secret. I hope we can start over like Ashley and I did. When you went through your drama with Mark, I didn't understand how you could lower your standards by marrying a bum, but you did. Ashley and I stood by and watched you ruin your life. Your sister died because of your stupidity, and I have learned to forgive you."

"You blame me for Ashley's death? Dad blames himself for her death, as well. What about you? What role did you play in her death?"

"I had nothing to do with her death, Sonia. Ashley and I made peace with each other way before she died. Because we went to counseling, we were able to heal some old wounds. Did *you* make peace with your sister? And as far as your father is concerned, he deserves to feel the way he does. He's the one who acted like she had a disease. She was molested by his fucking brother, and when we told him about it, he called her a liar. Did you know she was molested?"

"No, I didn't know until I read her journal. Did you know I was molested, too? I bet not. You were so caught up in trying to please Dad's mother, you didn't pay attention to what was going on in your home. Mom, the entire family needed counseling. Why didn't you suggest that I attend those sessions with you? Did Ashley not want me there?"

"Why didn't you tell me, Sonia, that boy was hurting you? I could have protected you. I was not trying to appease that bitch. I was trying to survive the brutal beatings your precious father used to give me."

"I didn't know Daddy beat you. You never told me. Why did you stay with him?"

"What else was I going to do? I didn't want anyone to know that I was stupid enough to let a man beat on me. I was supposed to be the intelligent one. I remember telling my friends I would never let a man put his hands on me. I was a fool."

"I'm very sorry you went through that shit with Daddy. You didn't deserve to be treated that way. You were a good mother and friend to Ashley and me. I just wish we knew how to communicate our feelings to each other. Every day I blame myself for what happened to Ashley, because it was my husband who killed her. He may not have stabbed her, but it was because of him that Sharon was involved in our lives. I made a bad decision by marrying him. I should have listened to you, and I am sorry.

"Did you know that Dad moved back to Puerto Rico and that Tina left him? He had a nervous breakdown and tried to take his life. He believes Ashley is haunting him."

"Well, your father is dealing with guilt, and I do not feel sorry for him at all. He knew what he was getting himself into when he got involved with that whore. She'll never let him see those kids. Anyway, I really called to wish you and Ajani well, and to see how you were doing. I have a few errands to make today and time is slipping away."

"I'm glad you called and we had a chance to talk. I love you, Mom."

I have not read Ashley's journal in a long time, and to be honest, I didn't want to anymore. The mystery about my sister was solved. Now it's time for me to find my babies.

Chapter 17

"Sonia, I have something to tell you. The news is a little disturbing, so please sit down," Alike said.

"What is it, Alike? It seems as if I can never have peace. What now?"

"Maritza escaped from prison and is looking for you. It seems as if she faked a seizure, and when they took her to the hospital, she slipped out through one of the back doors. She contacted Sheila and told her that when she got out she was going to find and kill you. You're safe where you are, so that's not a real concern for me."

"Well, I still need to call Mom and let her know about Maritza. Maritza may not be able to find me, but she might try to hurt my mother."

"But here's the other thing. Tracy is expecting a baby and believes Ajani is the father."

"Tracy told you that she is pregnant? She will try anything to get Ajani back in her life. The bitch was a little plump when she came to visit us. I bet you she was already pregnant then. She must really despise my ass. I wish she would just grow up."

"Well, I thought you should know. Are you going to inform, Ajani?"

"I'll tell him, but he's not going to be happy about it. Alike, you told Tracy that Ajani beat you when you were together, and I wanted to hear more about it. Ajani has never laid a hand on me, and I hope he never does."

"Sonia, Ajani is a different person now. When we were together, we did a lot of drinking and snorting cocaine."

"There is never an excuse for a man to abuse a woman, and I need to know what I got myself into by marrying him."

"If he has not shown you that side of him yet, then you have nothing to worry about. I believe people can change, and it's apparent he has. If he ever lays his hands on you, then you have to leave him."

"Let's talk about your wedding. How are the plans shaping up? Let me know if I need to do something."

"Planning for this wedding is stressing me out so much. Girl, I have to dye my hair every day to get rid of the gray hair that keeps popping up. Your wedding was much easier to plan, even though it was short notice. I'm getting the flowers imported in, and my dress will be ready in a few days. I know you said you didn't want to cater the event, but can you help me with the menu?"

"No problem. I would love to share my expertise."

"I'm not sure if Ajani is aware of this, and since you are his wife, you need to know that the doctor put Chelsea on bed rest. She was experiencing false labor pains a couple of days ago."

"I don't think Ajani knows. I'm sorry to hear about Chelsea's condition. I suppose the shock of Ajani marrying me has gotten the better of her."

"When Tracy broke the news to her, she fainted. She loved Ajani, and he broke her heart just like he broke mine."

"He has broken my heart, too, and I hope he doesn't do it again."

"If Maritza is not captured before the wedding, I'm going to hire security. I almost forgot to ask you about your trip to Montreal. Is it still on?" Alike laughed.

"You're a comedian. You seriously need to consider doing stand-up at the Apollo. I attempted to call Chris last week, but his number is disconnected, so I guess he moved on. Okay, Alike, it's time for me to let Ajani know what's going on. Thanks for always looking out for me.

I love you."

Sometimes I wonder why Alike is being so nice to me. She has really turned into a more caring person since she stopped using drugs.

"Ajani, I have some bad news to share with you. Tracy is pregnant and saying you're the father. Also, the doctor put Chelsea on bed rest. When was the last time you spoke to her?"

"That damn bitch is trying to play games with me! She sleeps around, so how in the hell can she say I'm the father? She will have to prove it to me, or better yet, have an abortion. I spoke to Chelsea two days ago, and she didn't tell me the doctor put her on bed rest. I know she hates me right now, but I told her that I would make sure she was comfortable until the baby is born."

"Tracy is not going to have an abortion. She is ready to be a mother, and is definitely going to term with this one."

"There is nothing for me to do, but wait and see. When the time comes, I will handle it. Who told you she was pregnant? I have a lot on my plate right now and can't deal with this shit."

"Well, you're going to have to deal with it, Ajani. You slept with the heifer. And you know I will never reveal my sources. Just know the bitch is walking around saying you are the father of her unborn child. I also found out the other bitch Mark was cheating on me with, Maritza, escaped from prison and is threatening my life again."

"You are safe here. A few of my investments went belly up, and I'm under a lot of pressure right now and the only concern I have right now is my baby. I am going to New York to see how she is doing. While I am up there, I will deal with Miss Tracy."

"When are we going to New York? And don't even think about telling me no. If you are concerned about Maritza, hire security to watch my every move. I don't want anything to happen to Chelsea or the baby, either."

"I would prefer you stayed out of it. When the baby is born, you will have ample opportunity to stay by my side. Chelsea is on bed rest because she is depressed. She is depressed because I married you. You would only make matters worse by going with me. I'll handle it, my love."

"You don't have a choice, because I'm going with you. As far as Miss Tracy is concerned, it's not time to deal with her. Why do you think she told Alike? Oops, I didn't mean to reveal my source. Anyway, it's best if Tracy comes to us first."

"Okay, whatever. I will be going to London for a meeting with my accountant this evening. Don't wait up."

"I love you, Ajani. Things will work out. Hey, don't make plans for tomorrow. I want to visit Jasmine."

"You'll have to go without me. I'm working on a major project that needs to be done before we go to New York."

He said a few of his investments went sour, but I think there is something else going on with him. And then to find out the crazy bitch Maritza escaped from prison. I'll never forget the last conversation we had.

She had the unmitigated gall to call me collect from prison to tell me how much she hated me. *Hey, Sonia, you think this shit is over? Don't think I'm going to allow you to live a normal life while I rot in prison. I don't think you ever realized how much I hated you from the very beginning. Mark loved me more than he wanted to admit. If Mark didn't love your ass, I would not be in jail. He trusted you, and that is the only reason he agreed to meet you at the zoo. I told him not to trust you. All Mark did was talk about how sorry he was for hurting your dumb ass.*

I get chills just thinking about what Maritza did to be with Mark. She killed Desmond, who was her boyfriend and my friend, and Mark's mother's friend, Red. I never understood how Maritza chose Mark over Desmond, a hard working man who loved her. She killed the nicest man I've ever known, and needs to rot in hell for taking his life. I have to be careful because Maritza had three years to plot, and now she is free to carry out her plans.

Chapter 18

Ajani came home this morning, screaming at the top of his lungs, "Sonia, we are going to South Carolina right now! Hurry up and pack! I don't have time to explain."

"I thought we were going to New York. Who's in South Carolina?"

"We are going to visit my father. I'll explain everything to you when we get on the plane. I'm sorry to have put you in this predicament. I tried everything in my power to keep our family safe. I don't have the time to go into details right now. We have to pack quickly before the officials arrive."

"What's going to happen to Jasmine?"

"Jasmine is going to be fine. Charles is going to send her to your mother's house."

"Did you speak to my mother?"

"I called last night and told her Jasmine's flight would be arriving in Atlanta tomorrow evening and that we would call her once we got to South Carolina. She told me to tell you that your nieces are in South Carolina instead of North Carolina. I told her I would look them up."

"Okay, well, can we talk and pack at the same time at least? I didn't know your father was still alive, much less living in South Carolina. How long has he been there?"

"Since you insist on talking and packing, I hope you are ready to hear all I have to say to you. There is a lot about me you don't know. I have not been entirely honest with you, and I am sorry. My mother and I escaped my father's wrath when I was thirteen years old."

"What in the hell is going on? What is your father doing in South Carolina? When did he leave Africa? Ajani, are you really African? Please tell me I have not married an imposter," I said with a slight chuckle.

"My parents are from Omaha, Nebraska. Mom is Caucasian and Dad is African-American. They met and fell in love while attending the University of Nebraska. Mom got pregnant with me in her senior year. Dad did the honorable thing and they got married. When Dad finished college, he had a difficult time finding a job as an accountant, so we moved to Norfolk, Virginia.

"According to my mother, things were cozy for the first ten years until Dad joined Uchenna, a religious organization. The name Uchenna means God's Plan in Swahili. This group was headed by a man they called King Aomar, who believed the group was chosen by God to free all African people from enslavement and to lead them out of bondage. King Aomar did not approve of interracial marriages and suggested my parents divorce. According to Mom, Dad had a difficult time choosing, because at the end of the day, he loved his wife and his son. He tried to separate his newfound religious beliefs with his home life. Of course, this caused major problems in our household. But, Dad bought into their principles and beliefs, and even took me to a few spiritual classes. We studied the Holy Bible, the Koran, and Mysticism to strengthen our spiritual minds and become one with God. I have good memories about those classes and the time I spent with my father. I haven't spoken about my parents in years, and this is real difficult for me, Sonia."

"I've never heard of this group, Uchenna. It sounds cultish to me. Why didn't you tell me about your heritage before? Does anyone else know about this?"

"No one else knows about me, Sonia. I've had to live this lie for several years because my mom and I were in hiding. Sonia, things changed drastically for us when Dad's status grew within the organization. He quit his job as an accountant with his firm and began working for Uchenna full-time as the chief advisor to the King. With this new role, Dad was at the King's beck and call, and this did not bode well with Mom. The King would call while we were on vacation or eating dinner, and Dad would have to leave and go to him. Mom was raised Catholic and did not believe in divorce, so she hung in there for three more years."

"I can definitely relate to your mother. I went through the same thing with Mark. He didn't join a religious group, but his addiction to drugs destroyed our marriage. So what was the final straw that broke the camel's back?"

"As you can imagine, Dad was living a double life in more ways than one. Uchenna believed in polygamy, and the King presented Dad with a young wife, his daughter Isoke, and she bore him two daughters. Dad was able to keep this a secret from my mother for two years. When Mom found out about his new family, she asked for a divorce. This infuriated my father, and he vowed to take me away from her. He said she was not capable of rearing an African child.

"I'll never forget that night, because it was two days before my thirteenth birthday. I remember hearing my father say, 'Don't even think about taking my son from me. Woman, he is an African prince and must remain with me. If I find out that you are planning to take my son from me, I will kill you.' This was the first time I saw my mother really afraid of my father. My parents fought from time to time, but it never resulted in violence. Mom was a really crafty woman, though, and we stayed with Dad until she came up with a plan of escape. I loved my parents and it tore me up inside to see them separate, but my father was in too deep."

"I can't believe what I'm hearing. This is right out of a movie. So your father was involved in a cult?"

"Sonia, we really have to get ready. We will discuss this on the plane."

"What's your real name?"

"My name used to be Terrance Coleman. My mom had our names

changed when we relocated. I don't want you to get the wrong impression about my father. He was a good man; he just got caught up."

"You love your father, but it sounds like your mother did the right thing by taking you away. How did you find out your father is living in South Carolina?"

"I hired a private investigator to locate him. I gave him a call last night and told him I needed to talk to him, so he invited us to his home."

"I know we are strapped for time, but I need to know why we have to leave England so abruptly."

"Sonia, we don't have time to discuss it right now. All I'm going to say is they have a warrant out for my arrest."

Chapter 19

After Ajani told me there was a warrant out for his arrest, I didn't say another word. What did Ajani do to cause the authorities to come after us like common criminals? Once on the plane, I called Alike to let her know we were going to South Carolina for a couple of weeks. She had a lot of questions for me that I could not answer.

"What's going on, Sonia? Why are you guys going to South Carolina? I didn't know Ajani had property there."

"His father is sick, so we are going to be there for a couple of weeks."

"I thought Ajani's father was living in Africa. Call me back when you can talk, because I know Ajani is there with you."

"Okay, I'll call you back. Please, don't tell Tracy where we are. I told Ajani about Tracy's allegations, and he's going to wait until she contacts him. Oh, don't tell Chelsea, either."

"I understand. Let me talk to Ajani for a minute."

"Alike, I need you to take care of Chelsea. Before my father fell ill, I was going to New York to hire a few servants to help her around the apartment. If Tracy is pregnant, give her money for the abortion. Tell her I am not going to be her meal ticket," Alike said.

"I know you can't talk right now, but I need you to call me as soon as you can. I need to know how to handle your affairs."

"I'll call you as soon as possible. Charles will be contacting you in a few days to transfer some of my bank accounts to your name. Charles is also going to put the house in England on the market. We think we have a potential buyer. Once the sale is final, Charles is going to retain twenty percent of the profit and send you eight percent. This money is to be used to take care of Chelsea and the baby."

"What's really going on, Ajani? Okay, how did the officials find out? What about the other homes?" Alike inquired.

"I don't want to go into details right now."

"No problem. I'll do whatever you need me to do."

It is evident to me that Alike and Ajani are hiding something from me because he went to the cockpit to finish his conversation with her. The stupid idiot put Alike on speaker and I was on the other side of the door listening to every word.

"Alike, I can talk now. That little bitch, Nima, got caught trying to blackmail some bigwig. She told him if he did not pay her, she was going to tell his wife that he likes to have sex with little boys. He, of course, went to the officials, and they set her stupid ass up. They told her they knew about our little escort business and wanted to know who was in charge. That stupid cunt gave them my name. How did she know about me, Alike? She told them I was the head of the entire organization. They came to my office two weeks ago asking me a lot of questions about my personal finances and my business. I told them I am an investor and didn't appreciate them barging in on me. Since they did not have a warrant, I told them to leave. Two days ago, they froze one of my smaller accounts and barged in on my accountant."

"I don't know how she could have found out about you. I do not discuss business with the workers. There must be a mole within our camp. Didn't Charles recommend her? I told him not to hire the stupid whore. I knew she couldn't be trusted. Did Charles close down the main office?"

"Charles responded quickly. He was able to get the computers and major files out of the office last night. When I spoke to him this morning, he told me the officials were there with search warrants. Charles was dressed in janitorial attire, so they didn't ask him a lot of questions.

He overheard them say they were on their way over to the house. They will be in for a surprise when they find out I'm not there. We were lucky this time."

"Whew! You are right about being lucky this time. We've made a lot of money together, and I don't want to end up broke. Did Tracy know about your dealings?"

"Of course not, and you should know that. I need you to lay low with the girls. I don't know how much that cunt said."

"I'm not worried. Were you sleeping with the bitch, too?"

"I slept with her a couple of times. I couldn't resist her big ass. We stopped sleeping together a few months before I got married, though. There is nothing like a woman scorned."

"I hope you learned your lesson, Ajani. These women are no good. Sonia is the best thing to have happened to you."

"I know. I hate this is happening to us right now. Did you know Henry and Mason got arrested in South Africa? They got busted sending a counterfeit check to a woman in New York who turned them in. Those knuckleheads did not cover their tracks."

"I heard about Henry getting arrested, but I didn't know Mason got caught, too. Let's hope Henry keeps his mouth shut, because you don't need to be associated with that crime, too. That's why I'm marrying a lawyer, because he is going to keep me out of trouble."

"My name better not come out of his mouth. He knows what I will do to him if he mentions my name. Remember his friend Robert Adeko?"

"Yeah, whatever happened to him?"

"Robert tried to blackmail me a couple of months ago, and I gave him an early retirement package."

"How do you know Nima is the one that turned you in? It could have been Henry or Mason."

"Henry might have, since Robert was his cousin. I know Mason didn't. In any case, I know you and Sonia have gotten closer over the last few months, and I must ask you not to tell her anything. The only good that will come from this mess is seeing my father."

"I didn't know your father lived in South Carolina. How long has he been living there? Is your mother with him?"

"My father has been living there for about ten years, I think. When my mother and I left him, he was living in Virginia. My mother died six years ago."

"Ajani, you and I used to be close, and you know how much I loved you. I would have done anything for you. It took me a long time to get over you. I hope you were able to open up to Sonia."

"Sonia is my soul-mate. I didn't tell her everything, but she knows about my father."

"Good, I'm glad you were able to open up to her."

"Alike, I loved you, too, but not in the same way I love Sonia. You and I were money-hungry drug addicts and not good for each other. If we remained together, we would have killed each other. You have been a good friend to Sonia and me. I know you know this already, but please tell the troops to hold off sending out emails, faxes, or letters until this whole thing blows over. Let me know when the money hits your account."

"Okay, but they are not going to be happy about this. This is really going to hurt our pockets."

"If I go to jail, no one will get paid again."

I could not believe what I was hearing. I didn't hear everything, but it sounded like Ajani admitted to being the mastermind of Alike's successful escort business and might be involved in some kind of email scam. I do not want to be considered an accomplice and wind up in jail, too.

Chapter 20

I saw the village nestled deep among the live oaks and palmetto trees as the plane landed. Colorful masked dancers and the music of cow-bells and drums greeted us as we emerged from the plane. I noticed goats and a rooster scampering across the land, and there were children everywhere. The multi-colored homes looked shabby, and I suddenly wondered where we would be sleeping. Ajani pointed to the huge home on the hill and said we would probably stay there. I did not get a good feeling about the place, but my husband assured me everything would be okay.

"Sonia, we will only be here for a couple of weeks. I can tell from the look on your face, you are not going to like it here, but it will only be for a short time. And due to the situation, it is best that we limit our calls."

"Ajani, tell me what is really going on. What are those statues over there? Are those pyramids?"

Before Ajani could answer me, his father appeared, looking very regal in a royal blue gown with a gold crown on his head. I felt like I was in the twilight zone.

His father cupped Ajani's hand and said, "My son, how are you? It has been too long. I am so happy God has allowed you to come back to me. This must be your lovely wife, Sonia. It is a pleasure to meet you."

"Yes, this is Sonia, and we are honored you would have us as your guests."

"My dear Sonia, you asked what these statues represent. Those statues represent our gods. We pray to them every day. Queen Mother will share with you our beliefs after you are settled. Ajani, all of this will be yours when I take my rightful place next to our former King Aomar."

"Dad, I don't think I could fill your shoes. How many people live here?"

"We have over five hundred people living at this location. We are having a retreat this weekend, and the rest of my members will be present to hear the message from God. Uchenna has grown tremendously under my leadership. We have communities in Detroit, New York City, Atlanta, Illinois, and Tampa. You could not have come at a better time. I will introduce you to the community on Sunday. In the meantime, let me introduce you to some of the family members. You remember Isoke my first wife, well she died during the birth of my third daughter. I remarried and this is my new wife, Queen Mother, and her children: Bashira, Bia, and Sakina. Isoke's daughters have grown up since you last seen them. This is Katungi, Naveli, and Baba. Aren't they beautiful?"

"It's nice to meet you, Queen. Your children are beautiful. How long have you and my father been married?"

"My son, it is so good to finally meet you. Your father and I have been married for six months. I've heard so much about you. Your mother should have never taken you away from your home. How is she doing?"

"Mom did what she had to do at the time. She died a few years ago."

"Son, let me introduce you to my other wives and children," his father said.

"How many wives do you have, Dad? I don't know how you do it."

"There is a lot I have to share with you, my son. I have sixteen wives right now. When King Aomar passed away last year, his wives became my wives. I had six wives at the time, and he had ten."

"How and where did you meet Queen Mother? She seems a little old to have children so young."

"She has been a true blessing to me. We met at a seminar I was facilitating in Brooklyn, New York. It was love at first sight. Her inquisitive nature reminded me of your mother. Those are the Queen's grandchildren."

"She is very beautiful. So how should I address you now? Can I still call you Dad?"

"Son, only you may call me Dad. Everyone around here calls me King Jelani. How did your mother come up with the name Ajani?"

"Mom's new husband renamed me. He was from Ghana."

"Was he a traditional African or a colonized one?"

"He was more European, if that's what you're asking. He was a professor at the university Mom attended."

"She went back to school? Did she complete her studies?"

"She graduated with honors and became a social worker."

I couldn't believe my eyes. I had to pinch myself. Ajani's father is the leader of a cult. I hoped and prayed silently we would not be here long. Queen Mother's children are very beautiful and resemble someone I know.

As I was staring off into space, Ajani told me Queen Mother wanted to show me to our room. I shared with him that I thought the kids looked familiar.

"I don't know much about her, but will ask Dad when we go to dinner. Dad said they met in New York. Maybe you all lived in the same neighborhood."

"Where are you all going for dinner? How come no one invited me?"

"Dad and I have a lot of catching up to do. I'm sure you understand. We won't be gone long."

I was definitely not comfortable with this shit , so I found a way to hide in the back of their van.

Chapter 21

Riding in the back of the van was so uncomfortable, but I was determined to find out what was really going on. Ajani is going to kill me if he ever found out that I've stooped to this level of snooping.

"Son, I am so glad you called me. How much trouble are you in?"

"Dad, I'm in a lot of trouble. I just need to lay low until it blows over. I'm not a king like you, but I do own a lot of companies."

"You know I loved your mother dearly, but we should have never married. How long was she sick?"

"Mom died of lung cancer. She was diagnosed with it two years before her death. It was a difficult time for me."

"I'm sorry I could not be there for her, but it was not in God's plan for us to remain together. I never meant to hurt her by being with Isoke. If it matters to you, I didn't love Isoke the way I loved your mother. Isoke blossomed into a wonderful woman and great supporter. She was King Aomar's firstborn, and he was devastated when she died. She bore him two children before she and I married. I miss her very much."

"Dad, there is something wrong with a father sleeping with his daughter. It's called incest. How could you be a part of an organization that condones such behavior?"

"The King believed the best way to keep the bloodline pure was to marry within. It may sound archaic to you, but we have been living this way for over thirty years and it has worked. I have decided to do things a little differently during my leadership. The King would not have approved of my marriage to Queen Mother because of her age. I am only supposed to marry women between the ages of nine and fifteen, but I fell in love with her, so I went with my heart."

"How did the King die? How did you get chosen to be the next in line?"

"He was eighty years old and died of natural causes. He was a great leader and father figure to me. When you and your mother left, I was his chief advisor, and when he gave his eldest daughter to me as a present, that moved my status up to High Priest, which made me next in line to be king. I would love for you to be my successor when I die. You don't have to answer now, just think about it. In the meantime, I have a gift for you, too."

"How old are you?"

"I'm seventy-five and my health is failing. I'm not as young as I used to be."

"Now, you have sixteen wives and you sleep with all of them? It must be nice to have all these women to choose from."

"My health is failing, but my stamina is still strong. My youngest child is three months old. You need to get a couple of wives, too, now that you are here. Isoke's oldest daughters are absolutely divine and great supporters of our way of life. One of them will be given to you as your wife. I am giving you the opportunity to choose one. Well, which one do you like?"

"Dad, they are my sisters and too young for me. Besides, Sonia would never agree to it."

"Young? They are in their twenties, Son, and they have not been married yet because I have saved them for you. Which one, Son? I think Naveli is the prettiest; she is my favorite."

"What do you mean she is your favorite? Do you sleep with your children? I thought you said you were doing things differently."

"They are not my children; they are Isoke's daughters. The only rule I changed was marrying Queen. Since you are my oldest son, I could not marry them off until you came back. So since you have returned to me, it is time for them to marry. The one you do not marry will become my wife. Naveli is more affectionate, and I give her to you as a present. I am going to build you a house on the compound, and Naveli can be your assistant or maid until you are able to get Sonia comfortable with her new lifestyle. Queen Mother will work with Sonia so that she will understand our way. She will adapt eventually. If you are not sure which one to choose, I'll send them both to your room tonight."

"I don't think so, Dad. Thanks for the offer, but I'm happily married. I promised Sonia I would remain faithful to her."

"I understand your commitment to your beautiful wife and apologize for offending you, but in the meantime, it is very important for you to learn about how we do things here since this is going to be your home. We are peaceful people, and my role as the leader is to make sure our members are empowered by their belief in the Father. Our children are educated in the European and Afrocentric models. It is important for our children to become doctors, lawyers, nurses, realtors, and teachers outside of this village. In order for us to educate all people from the African Diaspora, we must go to them. I would like you to review my financial statements and provide me with your thoughts. I think you will be impressed with how well we've done."

"Sure, I'll look at your finances. Why did you get involved with this group? Mom said you all were happy before you joined this cult. Our lives were disrupted because of this damn organization."

"Son, joining Uchenna brings me fulfillment in ways no one could ever imagine. I met King Aomar just as I was getting ready to enter a bar. He was preaching to all of the brothers about how the White man is continually stripping us of our manhood. I didn't feel like hearing him at the time, so I went inside of the bar. But then I heard him say that African men that marry White women are in denial and need to wake up before it is too late. I was offended by his rambling, and when I went outside to challenge him, he pulled me aside and said, 'Brother, I know your pain, and you will be set free once you remove the demon from your home.' This man did not know me, so how did he know I was married to a White woman? He invited me to a seminar he was having at his church the following evening. When I went, I met so many positive African men who embraced me and told me they loved me. I knew this was the place I needed to be."

"Mom was not a demon nor was she the devil. She was a beautiful woman that loved you. If you felt that way about her, how do you feel about me? I am part white."

"I'm glad your mother did not share with you what was really going on between us. We were not as happy as she led you to believe. We fought constantly, and our fights sometimes got physical. Your mother had an affair with a White co-worker and became pregnant. Due to the strain in our relationship, she ultimately had a miscarriage, and our relationship never recovered. I never forgave her indiscretions. Your mother took my love for granted and never understood or respected me as a African man. Do you remember visiting her parents in Nebraska?"

"No, she said that they died."

"Well, they did not die. When she got pregnant with you, they threatened to kill me. They begged her to have an abortion and to leave me. At first, your mother did not have a problem loving an African man, but then she grew to hate me when I could not find a job. She blamed me for our lack of finances. It was easy for her to blame Uchenna for the destruction of our marriage instead of herself. When I began sharing with her what I learned about being an African man, she disagreed with everything I said. She didn't believe that the pyramids were created by Africans nor did she believe that we came from kings and queens. She never understood the significance of our culture and our role in God's plan. The King's teachings helped me to see who the outsider was in our relationship and how she tried to oppress me as an African. It's very hard for me to discuss this with you, and I don't want to debate our beliefs with you. In time, you will understand."

"How could you say Mom was the oppressor? She loved you immensely. She left her family to be with you, Dad. Can't you see that King Aomar used you for his own purposes? I'm sure when I look at the financial statements I will see how much money you have brought to the organization. You were the one who changed, and I know people grow apart in relationships, but don't blame her because you chose Uchenna over your own family."

"Your mother was a White woman with privileges...privileges that were not afforded to me or even you. Our people have had to work extra hard to prove themselves, and we have to always jump through hoops just to be accepted. Your mother's people believe the myth about being the superior race. The superior race is the black race, but they want us to believe we are inferior to them. We come from kings and queens; our people built pyramids and invented many innovative things. Yet, we are made to feel inferior. You are a king, my son. Claim it."

"Dad, you married a White woman of your own volition. No one forced you to marry her. I am a product of the love you once shared."

"There is no excuse for my ignorance. I didn't understand the significance of my actions. Our parents vehemently opposed our nuptials, and we went against their wishes. Yes, you are a product of the love we had for each other, but it is important you learn the Uchenna's way so you can take your place as King. You may not understand this right now, but you will."

"Dad, I don't think I will ever understand or accept your views. However, I am willing to establish a relationship with you while we are here. I need this time to unwind and regroup, but stop trying to recruit me."

"Son, I know why you called me. You are wanted for illegally prostituting women and money laundering. I may live out here in the wilderness, but it doesn't mean I'm a fool. I know what you've been doing, Ajani. You say Uchenna is a bullshit cult, but how does it compare to you swindling people out of their money and selling sex and drugs? You are a predator of your own people."

"How did you know about my businesses? How could you know?"

"Son, I have friends in high places. Nothing escapes me. You think I didn't know where your mother took you? I could have taken you away from her a long time ago, but chose not to. King Aomar's dream revealed the exact day and time you would be calling me. Does Sonia know who you are?

"Yes, I told her before we left England. She doesn't know about the trouble I am in, though."

"Well, your secret is safe with me."

I regret not listening to my mother regarding Ajani. She told me to leave him a long time ago, but I refused to listen. I don't want to go to jail or even be associated with Ajani nor his father. I must find a way to escape this insanity.

Chapter 22

Queen Mother is a very interesting woman and looks good for being in her seventies. Her salt and pepper curly hair reaches the center of her back, and she wiggles when she walks. She speaks in whispers and often smiles when she talks about the King. She's only been with the group for six months, and I wanted to know how she got involved. She told me what she knew about the King's first wife, Isoke.

"Isoke was sixteen years old when she married the King. As you've heard the story, the King was married to Ajani's mother at the time. White people are the enemy according to Uchenna's doctrine; therefore, King Aomar told King Julani to divorce her. King Julani loved his wife and didn't want to end their relationship, so he lied to King Aomar and accepted Isoke as his wife. The women tell me that Isoke was a very obedient wife and never challenged her new husband. She gave him three daughters and also had two children with her father."

"That is some sick shit. How can you be associated with an organization that condones incest?"

"You are entitled to your European beliefs. We see things differently. As you know, I am very new to this organization, but can tell you they saved my life. When I met the King, I was going through a difficult period in my life. I was trying to raise my son's children on my own. My son is serving time in jail for raping and assaulting the twins' mother. When he got sentenced, his wife divorced him one day and got married the next to a military man. She felt it was best to leave the children with me because she wanted to start her life over. The rape took place in Virginia, and when I found out she was pregnant, I quit my job and moved in with her until the babies were born. She was like a daughter to me and she needed me. After the babies were born, she decided she wanted to go to law school, so I took the children with me to Tampa, Florida, where I purchased a home. It was hard raising four young children alone with no income. My home got foreclosed, and I had to rely on public assistance to survive."

"Your story sounds so familiar to me. Was their mother's named Ashley?"

"I rather not say it's still difficult for me to talk about their mother because her life was taken away brutally. I am the only mother these children know, and I want it to remain that way. I didn't blame her for not wanting to be a part of their lives."

I think I found my nieces, this is too much of a coincendence.

"What about the maternal grandparents? They could have helped you."

"The grandmother made several attempts to reach out to me when we lived in Florida, but I didn't want her pity. She wasn't there for her own daughters, and I didn't need her screwing up my babies."

"When did you leave Florida, and where did you go?"

"I had no choice but to move back to New York City. The children were older and the pay was better. I lost my job a year ago, and had to rely on public assistance and move into a homeless shelter. Living in the shelter stripped me of my womanhood and left me feeling irresponsible as a mother and grandmother. I was the only person these children had, and I let them down."

"You have been through a lot, but yet, you've remained strong."

"I wasn't always this strong. King Julani showed me how to love myself again. Here I am seventy two years old and it feels like I am starting my life over. King Julani conducted a seminar on "The Essence of a Woman". I was inspired by his presentation and felt my luck was going to change. He invited the women to his church to meet the rest of his group members. At first, I thought he was the reverend of a traditional church, but soon found out he was the leader of a community. The community sounded like paradise to me, and the Lord knew I needed him. He spoke openly and fondly about his own family, and I knew I wanted to be a part of his life. He was married for fifteen years, fathered eight children, and had twenty-five grandchildren. He stressed the importance of African unity and fathers being the head of our families. I didn't have a husband, but knew I needed someone to help me take care of my grandchildren."

"Did you think you were going to find a husband?"

"It seemed as if my life changed overnight. My son is an adult, and here I was raising young babies again. I had not been with a man in years, and was satisfied not having one until these children came along. Children need male role models in their lives, and when I first saw King Julani, I felt he was the one. I was tired of living in the shelter and I wanted to see the King again, so the children and I went to the church to hear him preach.

"The church was located in a two-story home in Brownsville, Brooklyn. When we entered the building, we noticed the beautiful African sculptures and paintings on the walls, and the scent of Egyptian musk was everywhere. We immediately felt at home when the family members embraced us with warm hugs and kisses. I was overwhelmed by the kind gestures and cried throughout the service. I was a devout Catholic since I was a child, but never have I experienced the feeling I had that day. King Julani told his members that God had a plan for our lives, and at that moment, I was ready to devote my life to him."

"Were you devoting your life to God or to King Julani?"

"Both. God brought me to Uchenna to become a queen. The King has changed so many of our member's lives. We did not know these people from Adam, but they opened their home to us. I chose to live with Brother and Sister Bele in their three-bedroom apartment in The Bronx. They had three small children. Brother Bele owned a video store and gave me a job as an assistant bookkeeper. Sister Bele was a stay-at-home mom. The Bele's mentored us in the ways of the Uchenna's.

"As I mentioned before, I was attracted to the King and determined to get closer to him. After each service, I made sure to talk to him, even if it was only for a minute. My story may sound sad, but it was God's intention for me to struggle a little bit so I could be prepared for the blessings he has in store for me. Despite the fact that King Julani has other wives, he spends more time with me. If King Aomar were alive, we would not have been allowed to get married because of my stature in the community."

"Queen Mother, it sounds like you have a very important role in this community. What does being Queen Mother really mean?"

"The role of Queen Mother is an integral part of our community. The King is our leader. He provides us with his vision, and I support him by making sure the women are successful mothers and wives. I am responsible for designing and implementing educational courses primarily for the women and children. I am also responsible for administering a special training program for girls who are ages eight through eleven. This program focuses on teaching these young girls how to take care of their homes, children, and husbands. We also touch upon polygamy families. As soon as they turn nine, they are sent to the King for seasoning. Once they are seasoned, the King and I select their mates. Our children are all doing well, and my grandchildren have adjusted to the Uchenna way of life. The children are in school right now, but if you would like, we could visit a few of the classes so you can get a better idea of the types of things they learn. Please note, the girls and boys do not attend the same school."

We went to visit the school for girls, and the first classroom we went into were for the five-year-olds. I almost cried when I saw those children. Some of the children were so skinny you could actually see their ribs, and their arms looked like toothpicks. The classroom was dirty and unkempt, with roaches running all over the place. I kept looking at Queen Mother to see if she noticed what I noticed, and decided she was brainwashed and didn't know what she was doing. When we went to the boy's school, you could see the vast differences in the quality of instruction and in the appearance of their classrooms. Some of the boys looked underfed, but overall, they looked vibrant and healthy. I made up my mind that I was going to call the authorities as soon as possible. They keep saying their principles are based on God's plan, and yet, I have not seen one Godly thing in this place.

"Queen, where are you from? You must be from another planet, because I can't believe you don't see the horrible conditions these children are living in. This is a cult, and you and all the members have been brainwashed."

"Sonia, Uchenna saved us from being homeless and hungry. I needed a stable place to raise my grandchildren. I am not brainwashed at all and can leave whenever I feel like it. I am not a prisoner here."

"You appear to be an intelligent woman, and I understand the complexity of your situation, but you do not need to subject yourself to this kind of life. Let me be clear with you, Queen, and I hope you don't take it the wrong way. If the authorities find out about what is going on here, you will be arrested. I know you understand what I am saying to you."

"Are you threatening me? I may appear to be naïve, but I can assure you I am not."

"I am not threatening you. I just wanted to make you aware some of these practices are considered child abuse and are illegal."

I think I went too far with Queen Mother, but there is something about her and those kids that makes me want to help them. I don't know how long it takes for a person to become fully indoctrinated into a cult, and I can only hope it's not too late for them.

"How did you and Ajani meet?"

"We initially met at a party, but I was not the one he was interested in initially. He dated my friend for a couple of months. At the time, I was having problems in my marriage. My former husband was a homicidal lunatic who had me running all over the country to get away from him. Ajani opened up his home to my family until my former husband was caught. It took sometime for me to fall in love with him, and when I did, it was all she wrote. Ajani and I have been together for three years, and we've just married. Ajani is pretty wealthy, so we have a couple of homes around the world. Our home in England is my favorite. I was born and reared in The Bronx, New York, and owned a boutique in Manhattan.

"I must admit I don't have a good feeling about this place, though. I think I would rather stay with my mother until whatever Ajani has gotten himself into is resolved."

"You and Ajani are now one, and that means you must remain by his side. We are not bad people, and you will learn many things from us. Well, it's our bedtime. I will show you to your room."

I thought a lot about what Queen Mother shared with me, and I had a serious problem with the girls getting married at the age of nine. Queen Mother apparently was brainwashed and incapable of seeing how wrong their practices were. Ajani needed to talk to his father about what they were doing or else he would find himself in jail.

By the time Ajani returned, it was about two in the morning, but I was up waiting for him.

Chapter 23

"Ajani, what in the hell is going on around here? Do you know your father is the leader of a cult? They believe in incestuous relations and having sex with young girls."

"Sonia, it's two in the morning. Why are you still up? I suppose you were waiting for me so you could badger me with one hundred questions. I told you my father and I have been estranged for several years, so I'm finding out a lot of things just like you are. We are not going to be here long, so don't worry your pretty little head about it. Let's get some sleep and we'll talk about it later."

Since I knew he was tired from hanging out with his father, I let him rest.

The next day, Queen Mother conducted a vegetarian cooking class. Ajani neglected to tell me that his father and his members were strict vegetarians. Queen Mother showed us how to make the perfect banana French toast with strawberries on top, curried vegetarian pasta, bean quesadillas, and creamy rice pudding without milk. I don't think I will give up eating meat, but I must say the food was very tasty. The one thing I noticed was only women attended the class.

"The women and children are kept separately from the men," Queen Mother said. "The only time men and women are together is to procreate and attend worship services. Our role as wives is to keep the house clean, cook the meals, wash clothing, and raise the children."

"Explain to me how polygamy relationships work. I've read about it, but never met anyone that actually practiced it. You are the primary wife, but you share your husband with sixteen other women?"

"Polygamy was the acceptable form of marriage in Africa prior to the arrival of the colonizers and Christianity. There are many single women raising children on their own, making life difficult. There are several advantages of having co-wives to help share the burden. We share the responsibility in raising our children and building a home for our family."

"What about friction between the women? I know you all must fight over the King's attention."

"The women don't like me because the King pays a lot of attention to me. After Isoke died, his second wife Jamila thought she would assume the role of Queen Mother, but the King selected me. When Isoke was Queen Mother, the King rotated between the women, but now he spends most of his nights with me."

"Aren't you afraid of one of these women harming your children? Women can be deceitful and vindictive."

"They are not stupid, and know that if they hurt my kids, there will be hell to pay. I'm in charge of all the women in the house, and they do as I say. You know Ajani is next in line to become king. Therefore, it is important for you to know your relationship with your husband will change."

"What do you mean my relationship will change? My husband and I do not prescribe to the concept of polygamy."

"Your husband is heir to the throne, and when his father passes away, I will become his primary wife. You will become secondary."

"I must reiterate, and please forgive me if I sound condescending, but Ajani and I will not partake in a polygamist marriage."

"I am not offended, Sonia, and I'm sorry if I offended you. I'm not sure if Ajani knows this, but our King is very ill and not expected to live much longer. Ajani will lead our people to the Promised Land."

"I'm sorry to hear Ajani's father is ill. What is wrong with him? And what are you talking about? What Promised Land?"

"Please don't tell Ajani what I shared with you today. His father has cancer of the liver and doesn't have much time."

"What if Ajani never came here? He would have to choose another one of his sons to be his successor."

"King Aomar had a direct link to God, and it was revealed to him that Ajani would return to his father. He told King Julani the exact date and time Ajani would return. We are a people that can see into the future, and our lives are planned around what we see. This power is given to us by Orishas, and it is important for us to remain in constant communications with them."

"What is an Orisha? How do you communicate with them?"

"Orishas are divine messengers, and we believe that each person's destiny is guided by a specific Orisha from birth. We communicate with them through prayer and sacrifices."

"Even though I do not attend church on a regular basis and believe in freewill, my belief in Jesus Christ as my Lord and Savior will not allow me to stay here. Ajani and I will be cutting our visit short," I said as I stomped off.

Chapter 24

"Ajani, we need to have a serious talk. I'm going to my mother's house. I cannot remain here with these people. Did you know they practice Voodoo and sacrifice animals?"

"No, I didn't know they practiced Voodoo or sacrificed animals. You are right; we need to leave here."

"Did you know your father is ill and wants you to become the leader of this cult?"

"My father and I discussed his desire for me to lead the group, but I declined. My father feels strongly about his religion, and it is his right. I am not going to dispute his beliefs with him. I made it very clear that I do not agree with his beliefs and would not replace him as leader when he dies. He has many sons who are capable of leading."

"I'm glad to hear you are on the same page with me. Queen Mother also shared with me that when he passes on, she would become your wife. I know you're trying to reconnect with your father, and don't want to stand in the way, but I can't stay here a day longer."

"My father and his followers are nut cases. Don't listen to anything they tell you. I think she was trying to fuck with your mind. You always let these simple bitches fuck with your head, and you need to stop allowing that to happen. I'm not going to participate in this archaic system. I understand now why my mother ran like hell from this man."

"When is Charles coming to get us? If he is unable to come tomorrow, I'm going to get on the next bus out of here."

"I spoke to Charles briefly last night, and he was on his way to California. I'll see if he can send the plane this weekend."

"That is three days away! I have to leave here now!"

"Sonia, I am a wanted man. We cannot just get on a commercial plane. You are my wife, and if they catch you, you will be detained.

"I'll tell you this, I reviewed his financial statements last night and he has made some really good investments. He invested in a lot of real estate properties in good markets. I can see where I got my business savvy from. He has set aside enough money to send all of the male children in the group to college."

"What about the women? Don't they get the opportunity to go to college? How do these women put up with being treated as second-class citizens? Your father makes me sick."

"Sonia, who are we to judge them for their beliefs? They are happy with their current situation, and we need to leave well enough alone. My father said it is the man's responsibility to take care of his family financially, and it is the woman's responsibility to take care of her man and the children. The women go to school up until the age of nine."

"Unbelievable! In this day and age, it is surprising to see women taking a back seat to their men."

"Don't I provide for you and Jasmine? You live like a queen, without a care in the world. How is that different from what they believe?"

"Are you saying because you are the breadwinner you have the right to oppress me? I hope that is not the point you are trying to make."

"I'm just saying it is the man's responsibility to take care of his family. Did you enjoy taking care of Mark? These women all appear to be happy, is all I'm saying. I don't want to argue about this. Let's go to bed."

❋❋

When I woke up the next morning, my husband was gone. *He didn't tell me he had something to do today.*

I decided I would not act ugly toward Queen Mother, and instead try to lead her back to Jesus. Maybe God sent me here to save them from themselves. *Once we get back to civilization, I'm going to find a church and join immediately.*

When I went to the Queen's room, she was praying, so I waited for her to finish before I entered.

"Good morning, Sonia. I hope you had a restful sleep. Will you be joining us today for our morning worship?"

"Good morning, Queen. I slept very well, and I hope you did the same. I will not be joining you this morning, but would like to talk to you about a few things. By the way, do you know where Ajani is?"

"Ajani and the King went downtown and will be gone for a couple of days."

"He should have told me they were going downtown. He knew that I wanted to get a bus ticket out of here."

"He told us this morning that you all are leaving on Sunday. The King asked him to join him at the last minute. I don't think he wanted to disturb your sleep. I must get ready for service. We'll talk later."

I was so pissed off, I wanted to kill someone. I don't trust these people. My gut tells me that Ajani's father is trying to prolong our stay here. If I have to walk one thousand miles, I am leaving this place on Sunday.

✦✦

Queen Mother informed me that Naveli was going with them. Naveli is very beautiful and my husband loves beautiful women. Even though he promised to be faithful to me, I don't trust him completely. King Julani is determined to make Ajani his successor, by any means necessary.

I could hardly wait until service was over to speak to the Queen and find out exactly where my husband was.

"Queen, I'm sorry for bugging you, but I need to know what the King is trying to do. I hope he is not trying to entice my husband with his own sister. Where are they going?"

"I really need to get ready for dinner, Sonia. King Julani owns a small bed and breakfast in Columbia, South Carolina, which is geared toward vegetarians. He thought the cozy environment would ease the stress Ajani was feeling. The King would never force Ajani to interact with his sister."

"I am going to follow them. I want to see you try and stop me. Why don't we go together?"

"I can take you there if you really want to go, but I don't see the point. Don't you trust your husband?"

"Ajani and I are working on trusting each other. He has cheated on me several times and I am not ready to completely put my faith in him."

"We'll go right after dinner. It is very important they don't know we are following them."

"How are we going to get inside the home?"

"I have keys. The house is tri-level and we'll hide out in the basement."

❖❖

When we got to the house, the lights were dim. We snuck into the house through the basement. Queen told me that the king installed a pretty advanced intercom system throughout the house and the basement is where it is located, so we would be able to hear their conversations.

"Dad, I like what you did with this home. Do you get a lot of customers?"

"Yes, we are the only bed and breakfast in Columbia that offers a vegan menu, and our products are environmentally safe."

"Well, let's get down to business. I want to make sure your finances and investments are protected when you pass. Do you have a will prepared?"

"Yes, Son, I've left everything to you. And since I've done that, I need you to be honest with me about why you are here. What happened in

England?"

"I operate an upscale escort business, and a few of my associates are involved with a few Internet scams. The British government is investigating the legality of my businesses."

"I thought prostitution was legal in Britain?"

"It is illegal to own a brothel, which I do not own. I own an escort business, which a close friend of mine manages. I believe I am being framed by some of my competitors. My women are some of the most beautiful in the world, and my competitors are unable to book clients. My business is legitimate and we do not sell sex; we sell companionship."

"I see you are no better than me, huh? How does your operation work? Are the women on the street corners selling their goods?

"No, my manager arranges parties for business owners to enjoy the company of nice looking women. We tell our women not to engage in sex, and if they do, we do not want to know about it. We provide medical insurance and a pension for our women."

"Maybe I should have thought about getting into that type of business. Well, I am sure your lawyers will get you off. In the meantime, what is going to happen to your business assets?"

"I took a couple of the accounts out of my name and transferred them over to my manager. They do not even know she exists, so my assets will be fine."

"Can you really trust this woman? I wouldn't."

"Mom did not have my name changed legally, so they will be looking for Ajani Omoro instead of Terrance Coleman. My friend needed to take care of a few ancillary items for me. Charles, my driver and business partner will remove her from the accounts once the transactions are complete."

"You are a brilliant business man. We need you to help us. God has a plan for your life, Ajani."

"I know God has a plan for my life. God has been very good to me. It seems to me that you believe in more than one God, though."

"We believe that God designated a few of his powerful spirits to watch over us in the way that Angels protect Christians. Now, let's talk about Chelsea. When is the baby due?"

"How did you know about her? You seem to know a lot about me."

"I know everything about you, and I know these Brits will hunt you down until you die. They will never stop looking for you, but if you remain with me, they'll never find you."

"Chelsea did not take my marriage to Sonia well. The doctor has placed her on bed rest until the baby is born. Before the shit hit the fan, I was on my way to see her. I'm determined to beat these allegations. I appreciate your kindness, and I guess I do not have a choice but to stay with you until this shit blows over."

"You have a choice, and it is up to you which path you decide to take."

"What choices do I have, Dad?"

"You can go to jail *or* you can accept your rightful place as my predecessor. In order for you to be respected, though, you must take another wife. Naveli would be the perfect wife for you, and has accompanied us on this trip so you can get to know each other."

"She is my flesh and blood, my sister, and I will not sleep with her. If I must have more than one wife, let me select my own."

"Naveli is not my daughter or your sister. It is our custom for you to marry my wife's daughter. This ensures our bloodline is pure."

"I must admit, Naveli is beautiful with her dark brown skin, wavy black hair, and slanted coal black eyes. She reminds me of a black China doll. It is going to be hard for me to look at this young tenderoni and not think of my first wife. I made a commitment to Sonia, but my Johnson has a mind of his own."

"Son, Naveli is yours for the taking. She gives awesome massages and will soothe all of your pain."

"Okay, Dad. I don't feel good about this."

"Naveli take Prince Ajani to the room upstairs and give him a massage.

The Queen and I looked at each other in disbelief as we heard this. I wanted to run upstairs and kick Ajani's ass. He promised to be faithful to me and now he is getting ready to make love to his sister.

"Sonia, let's go. You've heard enough."

"I want to kill him. How could he do this to me? I trusted him."

"Ajani is next in line to be king and these are our customs. Let's go now, before we get caught."

"I don't care if we get caught. Ajani has a lot of explaining to do. I promise to be quiet and not cause a scene."

"Okay, but I am going to turn off the intercom system. You do not need to hear their lovemaking. I'll turn it back on in the morning."

Chapter 25

I woke up to Ajani and the king talking about his rendezvous.

"Ajani, how are you doing this morning? Naveli did not disappoint me, did she?"

"I'm not proud about what happened, and I should have controlled myself. I promised my wife that I would remain faithful to her, and I've disappointed her again. Still, Naveli is an excellent lover; you taught her well."

"I am glad you approve. I will ask Queen Mother to make the wedding arrangements for you two."

"I said no. What happened between us will never happen again. I will not practice polygamy. What I did was wrong, and I will have to live with myself for what I did. I can only hope God can forgive me. Sonia and I will be leaving your compound this weekend."

"Son, please don't leave. I do not have much longer to live. I need you to lead the people. It is God's will for you to take your place at the throne."

"We are in the year 2005, and your belief systems are archaic. I think what you are doing to these people is a disgrace. You've brainwashed them, and I want no part of that. Let's go back to the house so I can be with Sonia. My dick always gets me in trouble. Alike and Tracy were both right about me. I'm unable to commit to one person. I do not deserve to be with Sonia. If I want this marriage to work, I must leave this God-forsaken place immediately. Excuse me while I call Charles to confirm his arrival. Please be silent, because I am going to put him on speaker, so you can be my witness."

"Charles, I've been trying to reach you for a couple of days. How is everything going? Send the pilot to pick us up on Sunday. Were you able to get the paperwork I need?"

"Ajani, I didn't know you were trying to reach me. I guess my phone is acting funny. I was getting a little concerned about you. I was unable to sell the house because the officials are holding up the sale until they can bring you in. I was able to transfer the major accounts into the name Terrance Coleman. By the way, I received a call today from a strange woman by the name of Maritza, inquiring about Sonia's whereabouts. Who is this Maritza person and how did she get my number?"

"Maritza escaped from prison and is looking to kill Sonia. What did she say to you?"

"She wanted to confirm Sonia's whereabouts. She claimed to be a very close friend."

"Were you able to transfer the smaller accounts into Alike's name? I want her to take care of Chelsea while I'm away. And have you heard from Chelsea?"

"I didn't put anything into that bitch's name. I suspect she is the one who called the authorities on you. Someone told me she is trying to start her own escort agency without you. She's been calling me everyday to find out when the money is going to transfer into her account. I am working on a few things, and the bitch is either going to disappear or wind up in jail. I have not heard from Chelsea. Would you like me to call her?"

"Yes, please call Chelsea and make sure she has what she needs. I do not want to lose this baby. Will you be here on Sunday?"

"I'm not sure. I'll call you on Saturday to confirm."

"You know I never trusted Alike. I would not be surprised if she is the one who set me up. There are a few more things I need you to do for me. Sonia has been a trooper through it all, and I would like to give her a gift. Please buy a diamond tennis bracelet for her. Also, I want you to locate buyers for the villa in St. Tropez. I want this to be a private sale."

"I'll take care of it, Ajani, or should I call you Terrance?"

"Call me Terrance. I almost forgot to ask about Jasmine. Did she arrive in Atlanta as planned?"

"She arrived to her grandmother's house with no problem. I told her grandmother you would call her as soon as you got to California. I hope that wasn't a problem. Would you like for me to stop in Atlanta prior to picking you guys up?"

"No, let her stay with her grandmother. I don't want to upset her anymore. Thank you, Charles, and I look forward to seeing you on Sunday."

"What would you like me to do about Maritza?"

"I almost forgot about her. Take care of it."

"I will! I told her I would call her back once I confirmed Sonia's whereabouts. She told me that they used to go to high school together and was looking forward to seeing her again."

"I'm sure she *is* looking forward to seeing my wife again. Find out how she got your number. It would be interesting to see how this all plays out. Keep me posted."

✳✳✳

"Dad, I'm sorry about going off on you. I do not want Sonia to ever find out what happened last night."

"Your secret is safe with me. I am sorry for trying to force you to accept your rightful position. Maybe in time you will see for yourself."

"I doubt it, Dad. Don't get me wrong, I embrace my culture and all its richness, but I don't agree with praying to different Gods and spirits. I may not be religious or an active participant in church, but I do believe in one God."

"Did your mother attend church when you were younger?"

"Yes, we were members of a Catholic church."

"When your mother and I were dating, she was faithful. One of the reasons her parents did not approve of me is because I was Agnostic at the time."

"That explains how you got caught up in a cult. You did not and do not know the Father for yourself."

"We are heading back to the house now so I can pray and ask God to show me who will be my successor."

"Good luck with your search."

I could not believe my ears. Ajani is a sick man. He has a lot more to worry about now. Because I know what kind of scumbag he really is.

"Queen, I'm ready to leave now, but I want you to take me to the airport."

"I can't do that. Sonia, I know what you overheard, but didn't you hear how much this man loves you. How could you expect him to choose between a naked woman and his commitment to you?"

"I most definitely expect him follow-through on his commitment to me. He promised to love, cherish, and respect me. I am going to have this marriage annulled."

"Don't be so irrational. It appears as if Ajani has made many mistakes in his life, but his love for you is apparent. Don't give up on him yet. I must ask you to keep what we did a secret. What we did is considered mutiny and is punishable by death."

Chapter 26

It took everything in my power not to bash Ajani over the head with a brick. It is hard for me to believe that the man of my dreams is a crook. I don't care what the Queen says; I am going to leave him as soon as we leave this place.

"Sonia, you were right about my father being a cult leader. The memories of my father were good, but they have been tainted by this experience. I can't stand what my father represents and wants me to do."

"What happened between you two? You seem a little tense."

"Dad tried to get me to sleep with my sister, Naveli. It's their custom for the daughter of the wife to be given to the eldest son as his wife. Naveli was with us last night, and he tried to force us to sleep together."

"How did he try to *force* you, Ajani? You are a grown ass man, and you know right from wrong. Did you make love to your sister?"

"No, I didn't make love to Naveli," Ajani lied.

"I told you these people are crazy. Your mother did the right thing leaving your father."

"By the way, Maritza called Charles inquiring about your whereabouts."

"She blames me for the death of Mark and her incarceration. I wonder how she got Charles' telephone number. I bet you Tracy gave it her."

"Either Tracy or Alike, and I hope you don't trust them. Alike cannot be trusted, Sonia. She only cares about herself, so don't be fooled by her sudden concern and like for you. She's never liked you, Sonia. I bet she never told you the extent of her friendship with Chelsea."

"Alike is a messy person, and the only person she has love for is you. I don't know who to trust right now. Can I trust you?"

"You can trust me, Sonia. I know I haven't been entirely honest with you, but I made a promise to love and cherish you. I guess this is a good time to tell you more about who you married, huh?"

"Ajani, we are husband and wife, so we need to be able to depend on each other. I should be able to share my fears, grief, and happiness with you. We are supposed to be best friends."

"You are an intelligent woman, so I'm sure you are putting the pieces of my life together. The escort business is legitimate and we do not condone sexual relations with the clients. I know some of the women do, but we do not openly condone it. Prostitution is legal in Britain, but there are some rules that must be followed. Someone informed the authorities that our agency was in fact a huge prostitution ring that launders money for criminals. I must admit, I have looked out for a few of my friends as they have for me in the past, but nothing major."

"Money laundering is illegal. What is Alike's role in all of this?"

"She is the front person. She hires the women and supplies them to our clientele. Our clientele are big-time executives of major corporations. My plan was to transfer a few accounts over to her until I was cleared."

"But you can't trust her, so what are you going to do?"

"Charles is the only person I truly trust to handle my affairs in England. He believes that Alike set me up so she can become a major player. Needless to say, we did not transfer anything into her name and she is extremely pissed off right now."

"Wow! So did Charles transfer the accounts in his name? What is going to happen to our homes? Where are we going to live, Ajani?"

"No, we are using my birth name, Terrance Coleman. Charles was unable to sell the house in England, and if everything works in our favor, we will be living in California. No one will find us there, I assure you."

"What are we going to do about Maritza? Tracy probably told her where my mother lives. I can't believe this shit. I am so tired of running."

"Charles is going to take care of it."

"What is he going to do? He doesn't even know where the bitch is. Have you spoken to or heard anything about Tracy? How is Chelsea doing? I know I'm rambling, but it's only because I'm afraid."

"No, I have not spoken to Tracy nor am I going to. I don't know how Chelsea is doing. I told Alike to take care of her, but I could care less about those bitches."

"Once you are cleared, what are you going to do about the agency?"

"The escort business is lucrative, but it's not my primary source of income. I'm willing to let this escort business go and start another agency under a different name. There is a lot of money in companionship."

"Give it up, Ajani. Did you ever purchase the nightclub in Miami?"

"No, I didn't purchase the nightclub. When we move to California, I could revisit the idea. If you still want to open up the clothing store, I'll make all of the arrangements."

"What's going to happen to us? It's like I have a curse on my life. It has been three years since I last seen or heard from Maritza, and I would have thought she would have moved on by now."

"Why should she move on? According to her, you took her life away. Don't worry about her, Sonia, because Charles is going to take care of it."

"Maritza should have left Mark alone and stayed with Desmond. This woman had two beautiful daughters and was attending college, and she threw it all away."

"Mark must have been something else to have all you women dying for his attention."

"Mark was a needy person. He grew up without a mother, and when she was around, she was on drugs. He did the best he could under the circumstances. I made the mistake of thinking the love I had for him was enough to save him."

Chapter 27

"Mom, how is Jasmine doing? I'm sorry I took so long to call you."

"Are you okay? I've been so worried. Jasmine is fine and concerned about you, too. Charles told me that you were unable to receive phone calls."

"This place is crazy. Ajani's father is a cult leader. I'm glad we did not bring Jasmine with us. His father calls himself King Julani, and he has sixteen wives. His first wife is called Queen Mother and she is seventy-two years old, but looks forty. She joined the group six months ago with her grandchildren. The twins look like they could be Ashley's"

"Where is Queen Mother from?"

"She's from New York. I think she told me that she lived in Brooklyn. I can't put my finger on it, though. There is more to Ms. Mother than meets the eye. I hope I will be able to get her to share more about herself to me before we leave. Has Tracy tried to call you?"

"No, she knows better. Do you want to speak to your daughter?"

"Not right now, Mom. I have to go. We are leaving in two days. We'll call you when we get to California."

"Sonia, you should not treat your daughter this way. What is your problem? Didn't we have a long discussion about this already? Do you remember calling me a bad mother because you claim I was not there for you? How do you think your daughter feels right now? She is worried sick about you. I'm going to put her on the phone right now."

"Mommy, how are you and Dad doing? Charles told me that everything was going to be okay."

"We are fine, dear. We are visiting Daddy's father who is ill. We've been going back and forth to the hospital, so we haven't had the chance to call you. I have so much to tell you about my trip to California, but Mommy has to go now. I love you."

"I love you, too, Mommy. Please be careful, and give Daddy a hug for me."

It hurt to hear my daughter's voice on the phone. I didn't realize how much I missed her. Once we get settled in California, we'll send for her.

Tracy and I have some unfinished business to take care of. I know she gave Martiza Charles' number, and I can't believe she hates me so much that she wants to see me dead.

"Hi, Tracy. I'm calling to see how you're doing. I know we've been at each other's throats lately, but our friendship should be able to withstand anything. I feel bad about the last conversation we had."

"Don't feel bad, Sonia. It's all good. You've always been a trifling bitch. How's everything going for you? Is Ajani in jail yet?"

"Why would he be in jail? He did nothing wrong. Is there something you need to tell me?"

"Not really, but Alike said there is a warrant out for his arrest. I told you he was not a legitimate business man. Alike said you guys are in South Carolina, so where are you exactly?"

"We stopped in South Carolina for an hour and then we moved on. I'm not at liberty to discuss where we are now. It seems as if Alike has done a good job of keeping you abreast of my affairs. So I hear you are pregnant and think Ajani is the father?"

"I knew the bitch couldn't keep her mouth shut. Does Ajani know?"

"Yes, he knows about your alleged pregnancy, and he is not happy about it. What are your plans?"

"I'm going to keep the baby with or without the assistance of Ajani."

"Why did you sleep with him? I thought you were over him. How could you betray me, Tracy? I thought we were friends. I've learned many surprising things about you through Ashley's diary."

"Sonia, I've been upset with you for a very long time, ever since high school to be exact. Because you are self-centered and consumed with your own issues, you neglected to notice the pain your sister and I endured. I remember the time when I tried to tell you I was pregnant, and all you wanted to talk about was finding a place for Mark to live. When I attempted to tell you Ashley was doing drugs, you didn't hear me because Mark had a fight with his mother's boyfriend. You never listened to anything anyone else had to say. I vividly remember the day as if it were yesterday, when I told you about my acceptance into Bronx Community College and that I didn't have the money to go. You never congratulated me, but you made sure to mention to me about you leaving for college in a couple of days. Sonia, your parent's didn't have money to send you to college, either. Still, you found a way to get your education paid for, and did you bother to share that information with me? No, but you made sure to tell Mark. I even wrote while you were in college, and you never wrote back. It was like you left The Bronx and said to hell with everyone else."

"Wow, I never knew you felt this way about me. I don't even know where to begin. You're right; I was consumed with what was going on with my own issues, and maybe it was apparent that I was not a good friend or sister. As I recall, you were caught up into being the best dressed and most popular, and didn't seem to care about going to college. We never talked about your aspirations, and whenever we did, you seemed uninterested. When you needed a place to stay, didn't I beg my mother on your behalf? There were things you never shared with me, and I didn't hold that against you. I thought when we reconnected all was forgiven, but I guess not. I had to learn how you really felt about me from Alike and by reading my dead sister's journal. You and Ashley meant the world to me, and I was extremely thankful for everything you did for me when Ashley was killed."

"You took Ajani away from me, and you knew I loved him. I never expected you to establish an intimate relationship with Ajani because I chose to be with Sheila. What happened to the unspoken rule of not dating your friend's boyfriend? You did me dirty, Sonia, and after all I did for you. The only reason he opened his home to you was because of me. Did you ever thank me for saving your life? That's why I'm going to have his baby, and regardless of what you say to me, he is going to take care of his responsibilities."

"I see now where you are coming from, and I'm sorry it had to come to this. But, I need you to get one thing straight; I *did not* take Ajani from you. You had one year to get your shit straight, and you blew it. Is it my fault you were confused about who you wanted to be with? I'm afraid not, Missy. You're always quick to point out my flaws, but what about you? You called me naive, dumb, and stupid for being with Mark. We loved each other, and I think that is why you were jealous. You say you loved Ajani. When? Did he know that? I doubt it, because you are incapable of loving anyone. You used Sheila and Ajani for your sexual pleasure, and now you want to blame me because he will not acknowledge you. I hope you will be able to at least show love to your baby. You have a lot of growing up to do, and I hope you do so before the baby is born. And I would be remiss if I did not ask you about Maritza. Did you give her Charles' number?"

"I have never lied about who I was or am. I told you before that I'm the daughter of a pimp and whore, and have had to work for everything. There was no one showing me love at all. My parents did not love me the way your parents love you. Did you treat your mom, right? Hell no! It pained me to see the pain you caused her when you went to go live with your father. I secretly wished she would allow me to live in your place. You had it made, Sonia, just like you do now. You don't fucking deserve the life you are living right now. When Ashley was selling her ass and using drugs, I was there for her. Where were you? You were so caught up in Mark and his bullshit that you sacrificed the life of your sister. So, don't say a damn thing to me about flaws. You say I have not shown love to anyone. Well, you are mistaken. I loved you, Sonia, and have always been there for you. What in the hell did you sacrifice? You are alive and Ashley is dead."

"I loved you like a sister, Tracy. I may have been self-consumed with my own life, but you were a part of me. If I had known you really loved or wanted to be with Ajani, I wouldn't have started a relationship with him. You were there for me when Ashley died, and you made sure my family was safe. I am forever indebted to you."

"I was wrong for sleeping with Ajani, and I'm sorry. Unfortunately, I can't change what happened. In response to your question about Martiza, I didn't give her Charles' number. Alike gave her the number. She's not your friend, and you are stupid for believing she cares about you. So where do we go from here?"

"I don't know where we go from here, Tracy, but I wish you the best of luck with your pregnancy. Please take care of yourself."

"Tell Ajani I would like to speak to him. This pregnancy is not going away, and I will need his support."

"I'll tell him, but as I said earlier, he does not believe the baby is his. So, you're going to have to take a DNA test to prove otherwise."

"Well, you have not heard the last of me, Sonia."

"Tracy, cut out the dramatics. If he is the father, he will more than likely take care of you as he is doing for Chelsea."

"He's not taking care of Chelsea. Alike is still waiting for him to send the money he promised. Is homeboy running out of money?"

"You and Alike are some messy bitches. I can't speak to the agreement he made with Alike."

"Whatever, bitch! Tell Ajani to call me when he's ready to discuss how he is going to provide me with medical assistance."

"Ajani is not your meal ticket. When the baby is born, he'll pay for the DNA test," as I slammed the phone down in disgust.

The heifer is a piece of work. The bitch was probably hoping I would tell her where we were located. I'm not convinced Tracy has not been in contact with Maritza. Therefore, I'm going to tell my mother to be on the lookout for the deranged bitch.

Chapter 28

After my exchange with Tracy last night, I was ready to tear into Alike's ass.

"Good morning, Alike. How are you doing this wonderful morning? Before I forget to tell you, we will not be able to attend your wedding."

"I'm so glad to hear from you. How is everything going, and are you guys going back to England? Oh, and you don't have to worry about the wedding. It has been cancelled. I caught David sleeping with one of the girls two days ago. I will not put up with cheating. I'm not like you and Chelsea. By the way, she had a baby boy last night and named him Ajani Jr. When will Ajani be coming to New York to see his first son?"

"I'm sorry to hear about David. I know you were looking forward to getting married again. And I don't know when we are going back to England. We are waiting for a suitable buyer for the house, but I'll let Ajani know about his son."

"Let Ajani know I have not received my money yet. Chelsea's medical expenses were pretty steep."

"I'll relay the message to him. Alike, why did you give Maritza Charles' number?"

"What are you talking about? I don't even know Maritza."

"Whatever, Alike. I know you gave the number to Maritza. We're also aware you are trying to take over the business. I will not allow you to run my husband's name into the ground."

"I do not appreciate your tone, Sonia. What are you talking about? You should know I wouldn't do anything to hurt you. Where is all of this coming from? It sounds like you've been talking to Tracy."

"Alike, I know you are looking to branch out on your own."

"Did Ajani tell you he was supposed to give me full ownership of the business six months ago?"

"No, he never mentioned anything about handing the company over to you. Still, you had no reason for setting him up. Now the business is in jeopardy of shutting down, and you will end up with nothing."

"No, *you* will end up with nothing, because Ajani is going to go to jail. Ajani will pay for everything he has done to me."

"What did Ajani do to you? He made sure you were financially set by allowing you to manage the business. He paid for your rehabilitation *and* the condominium you and Tracy are living in."

"The hell he did! Ajani didn't pay for shit. I make all of the arrangements and hire all of the ladies. All he does is collect the checks. He shouldn't get anything for my labor. When Ajani and I were together, he used and abused me, and he agreed to give me the business for my loyalty."

"You will not get away with this, Alike. I'll feel sorry for you when this is all settled."

The whore played me all along. I should have known the bitch was up to no good.

✳✳

"I hear you and Ajani will be leaving in a couple of days. I wish you would give us an opportunity to help you. You all are safe here; no one can find you," Queen Mother stated.

"Ajani and I do not agree with some of your practices, and we feel it would better for us to leave. You said Uchenna saved your life by providing you with the assistance you needed to raise your children, and that is good."

"At first, I didn't understand or relate to some of Uchenna's beliefs, but I've come to appreciate how my life has changed because of them. As you know, we practice polygamy, and you seem to be uncomfortable with it. Our customs are based on the matrilineal system, which means the children belong to the same descent group of their mother. So, it is not unnatural for the father to claim his wife's daughter as his wife or for his sons to marry their mother's daughter. This practice is not uncommon in the world. The Minangkabu of West Sumatra, the Nairs, Bunts, and Kurihiyas of Kerala, India, the Khasi and Garo of Meghalya, India, the Naxi of China, and the Gitksan of Britain all follow this system."

"I've never heard of these groups, and it sounds primitive to me. Your rhetoric is full of nonsense, and you will not convince me it is okay for a father to sleep with his own daughter. And it is a crime for adults to engage in sexual intercourse with minors. Are you willing to allow your granddaughters to marry a grown-ass man?"

"Our goal is to educate and uplift our African brothers and sisters. I know you think the King is some kind of pervert that gets his kicks out of sleeping with young women, but he is not. He preaches about love and responsibility. King Julani is our spiritual father, advisor, and leader. He was selected by God to interpret God's plan for our lives and our contribution to the world. Unlike King Aomar, King Julani goes into the community to spread the word, and brings the priests and priestess with him to recruit new members. We also conduct seminars on healthy eating and living."

"You mentioned previously about you and the King selecting mates for the young women, and how the women don't interact with their husbands except to engage in sexual intercourse and to eat. What about the children? Are they separated from their mothers, too?"

"Yes, the children are separated from their mothers at the age of five. When they reach five, they enter a boarding-like school and are grouped by age. There is a lead mother who provides lessons and watches over them. It is very important for the children to be on the same page. I don't want you to think they do not spend any time with their mothers, because they do."

"I guess the biggest problem I have with your group is how women are treated. Nine is too young for a child to get married or be with adult men."

"What age did your menstrual cycle begin?"

"My period began when I was about nine or ten years old."

"Menstruation represents womanhood in our society."

"Child marriage is a violation of their human rights. These children are not old enough to give their consent, which means they are forced into a situation beyond their control. I can't believe a woman of your intelligence thinks this behavior is acceptable. These children are not psychologically, physically, or sexually mature to be married. You are just as despicable as the King, and when they arrest him, I hope they do the same to you."

"These are our customs, and I will not apologize to you or anyone regarding them. These children are safe and well taken care of here. In today's society, our children are forced to be left alone because their parents are working, and then they are unable to connect with their children when they come home because they are too tired. Our children have the entire community looking after them. We do not have to deal with some of the issues plaguing children today like drug abuse, promiscuity, crime, and depression."

"You must be kidding me. You can't be serious. The only people benefiting from this crazy set-up are the men and the King. I am no feminist, but I do believe that women should have the opportunity to become educated beyond the age of nine and choose their own mates. Didn't you choose to be with the King? Is the King going to initiate your granddaughters, too?"

"As I said to you before, you don't have to accept our ways as your own, but please do not judge us.

Chapter 29

This is our last day here, and I can't wait until we finally leave this place. I overheard Ajani's conversation with Charles last night, and it seems as if Alike has been picked up by the police.

"I bet you the bitch ain't laughing now. I wish I could have seen her face when the police broke down her door. She definitely was not prepared for this shit. And since her bank accounts are frozen, she will not be able to make bail. I told her not to fuck with me," Ajani said.

Alike deserves everything coming to her. I decided to rub salt in Tracy's wounds by giving her a call.

"Hey, Tracy, I hear your best friend has been locked up. What happened?"

"Why don't you tell me, Sonia? You and Ajani think you're safe and sound. I wouldn't have a party just yet, though. She's not going to be in jail too long. Alike shared everything with the police and told them where you are. Ajani will not be able to pin this one on her."

"Firstly, Ajani has not committed a crime. It was Alike's job to make sure the women did not solicit their clients for sex."

"There you go being a dumb ass again. Sonia, Ajani is into more than just prostitution. Alike and Ajani are being investigated for drug trafficking and Internet fraud. The authorities will grant Alike immunity for her cooperation. Ajani and Charles are going down for all of their misdeeds. Oh, by the way, they found Maritza. Sonia, your storybook life is about to be over."

"Charles and I are innocent bystanders. They have nothing on me."

"Charles is more than a driver, Sonia. Charles and Ajani are partners. Did you ever figure out who gave Maritza Charles' phone number?"

"I confronted Alike about it, but she denied it."

"Well, she gave her the number in hopes that Maritza would kill you."

"I'm so sick of you damn women. Where did they find Maritza?"

"They found her dead in the restroom of a bar. Alike believes Charles poisoned her."

"She's in a better place now."

"Charles, not Alike, is the one setting Ajani up. Charles is the mastermind behind it all. He alerted the authorities about the inner workings of the company."

"You're crazy! Alike is playing with you, Tracy. She wants to instill fear and distrust between Ajani and Charles."

"Alike is going to tell them about your plans to go to Santa Barbara. You will get an opportunity to see what it feels like to live in jail. You see Miss-Know-It-All, Charles contacted Alike a few months ago and asked her if she wanted to work with him because he was breaking away from Ajani. He said Ajani had gotten careless and sloppy. He offered her a higher percentage of the money for a price. She had to work with him on getting Ajani out of the picture. The plot was to have one of her girls contact the authorities in the United States and give them details about a drug shipment headed for New Jersey. Ajani thinks the officials are investigating the escort business, but they're not. Charles is scheduled to pick you guys up tomorrow, but guess who else will be on the plane? The only reason I'm telling you this, Sonia, is because I still have love for you. We've been through a lot together. I was wrong for treating you like shit and not telling you about Ashley. I also want to apologize for sleeping with Ajani. It was only done out of spite; I did not want to see you happy. My only advice to you is to get out of there now."

"I'm sorry for not being there for you and Ashley. I love you, Tracy, and never wanted our friendship to end over some nonsense. How are you doing otherwise?"

"I'm definitely pregnant, and I am happy about it. I really want to be a good mother to my child, but don't know how. The one thing I know for certain is I'm going to make sure my child has the kind of love I never received when I was younger."

"I'm happy for you in a strange way. Are you sure Ajani is the father?"

"I'm pretty certain, but I won't know for sure until the baby is born."

"How are Chelsea and the baby doing?"

"Chelsea moved out of the condo and into her parent's home in Long Island. The baby looks a lot like Ajani."

"I must alert Ajani about this as quickly as possible, and we don't have much time to come up with another plan."

As I hung up the phone, Queen Mother was waiting to talk to me.

"You seem a little disturb. What's going on?"

"We are in a lot of trouble. I am sure the King did not share with you about the trouble Ajani and I are in. But, it looks like our cover has been blown. Ajani's partners have set him up and the authorities will be here tomorrow."

"Sonia, I thought a lot about what you and I talked about the other day, and I want to thank you. I don't want my grandchildren to be subjected to the type of abuse I see going on around here. I'm so surprised at myself for allowing this to go on. I will help you to escape this place. I must share something with you, though, and it's not going to be pleasant."

"What now? My life has had so many ups and downs, I'm prepared for anything."

"Isoke, the King's first wife, was murdered. She wanted to leave the compound, and the King found out and had her disposed of. It is a crime to leave this place."

"Isoke grew up in the community, so why did she decide to leave?"

"It seems as if she befriended someone who used to be involved with Uchenna when she went downtown to go shopping for food and clothing. The women are allowed to go downtown once a month. The woman gave her some literature about cults and told her if she wanted to leave to contact her in a month. Every time Isoke went into town, she would see this lady and eventually was convinced to leave our group. Isoke had an escape plan and everything, but the King found out and had her killed. All the women were banned from going downtown by themselves for months. The King decided last week he would allow us to go again. We are scheduled to go downtown next Friday, and I'm going to see if I can take the grandchildren with me."

"We can come up with a plan for you to leave with us, but it might be risky. I am afraid for you, Queen Mother. There is something about you that makes me want to help you out of this situation. I guess because you lost a daughter-in-law and I lost my sister. What was your daughter-in-law's name, again?"

"Her name was Ashley. When I look at her daughters, I see her sweet and innocent face. These children were not born out of love because their father raped their mother. All I ever wanted to do was make everything perfect for their lives. I knew who you were the moment I laid eyes on you."

"Oh my God, your name is Rita! These children are my nieces. I had a strong feeling you were the Rita, my sister was referring to in her journal."

"When you asked me if the twins mother's name was Ashley, I purposely did not answer you."

"Why would you leave me in the dark for this long?. Ashley's former girlfriend sent me her journal and that is how I know about you. Ashley never mentioned you or the children before she died. My mother just told me Ashley gave birth to twins and that she lost contact with you. It was my plan, before we left England, to look for you. God is real, and I am so thankful he has led me to you all. We must get out of here as soon as possible, before these children become so entrenched into this society it will be difficult for them to recover. I need to ask you this question again. What was your relationship with my mother?"

"Your mother is an interesting lady. You read Ashley's diary, so you know how she came to live with Raul and me. I found her reaction to Ashley's disappearance really strange. When I called to tell her Ashley was safe and that I would gladly send her home the next day, your mother told me not to. I would have never allowed my daughter to run the streets the way she let Ashley. Ashley had too much freedom and no accountability. I understood months later why Ashley hated your father, but I never understood the relationship she had with your mother."

"My mother claims Ashley and I were disobedient, and she was tired of fighting with us. I guess she took the easy way out. I must admit, I took the easy way out, too, with my own daughter. When I was hiding from my husband and his crazy girlfriend, I allowed my daughter to live with Ajani, and I didn't know him from Adam."

"That is an entirely different situation. Your life was in danger, and you really didn't have a choice. Your mother had a choice, and decided to let someone else raise her child. Your mother was enjoying the single life and you all got in the way. Your mother never gave me a dime for Ashley or these children. These girls do not even know she exists because they were toddlers when they last saw her. She convinced Ashley to forget about her own children and move on with her life. Ashley did not want me to raise her children at first because she wanted to really be a mother."

"I had a feeling my mother wasn't telling me the truth. Well, I can't do anything about it now. My main concern is for the children. We have less than twenty-four hours to get our plan together. Rita, I want to thank you for taking care of Ashley and her beautiful children."

"Ashley meant the world to me, and I considered her my daughter. These are my grandchildren and I love them dearly. What my son did was wrong. I can't change how they were conceived, but it is my wish they never experience the pain their parents endured as children."

"Raul was in pain? What happened to him?"

"I am originally from Panama, and growing up there was wonderful. I have such fond memories of my time there, and often times, I want to kick myself for disappointing my parents by getting pregnant so young. My parents were both teachers and strict, but loving. They had four children; three girls and one boy. I'm the youngest girl, and my baby brother Raul died in a car accident when he was thirteen years old. My two oldest sisters became teachers and are still living in Panama. We are not close at all, and they consider me an outcast."

"How old were you when you had your son?"

"I was nineteen, dumb, and in love with a boy that lived up the street. My parents tried to tell me he was not good for me and I should concentrate on my schoolwork. I was in college at the time, studying to become a medical doctor. But, I loved Mateo so much and could not hear them. Mateo was two years older than me and really handsome. Raul looks a lot like his father. We were dating for about three months, when I got pregnant. My father was so furious, he told Mateo's parents he had to marry me. We had a shotgun wedding, and that's when the horror began for me.

"My father bought our first house and helped get Mateo a job at a car shop. Mateo and I lived together for five years before I had enough. Mateo was physically abusive to me, and because of our custom, I never told anyone. He would beat and rape me constantly. I lost many babies because of his abuse. The only reason I left him was because he threw Raul down the stairs and broke his arm. That's when I left Panama and moved to the United States with my aunt, Lora. My Auntie Lora lived in The Bronx. She helped with Raul and convinced me to go back to school to get a degree. It is with her help I was able to finish college. Ashley reminded me of myself, and I knew I had to help her. Your mother pushed her aside, as my parents did to me."

"Rita, when we get out of this place, I want to be a part of my nieces' lives."

"Of course, they need to know other members of their family."

My mother is a piece of work, and I'm determined to change the way I feel and act toward my daughter. Reading Ashley's journal has given me a sense of peace in ways I would not have imagined. My only wish is that she could be here now so I could tell her how sorry I am.

Chapter 30

"Sonia, you have to leave there now! The police are planning on raiding the place at midnight. Alike is out on bail, and has provided the authorities in England and the United States with the information they need to prosecute Ajani."

"Thanks, Tracy, for giving me the heads up. I guess Charles posted Alike's bail, huh?"

"Yes, he flew in last night. I overheard them talking when they came in. Charles is supposed to call Ajani in a few minutes to confirm his flying into South Carolina tomorrow evening. Did you tell Ajani what I told you?"

"No, I didn't get a chance to. I found Ashley's children, and I want to take them with me."

"You need to tell him. Also, the authorities know Ajani's real name is Terrance Coleman. Charles provided Alike with the documentation."

"Where are you now? I hope you're not calling me from Alike's home."

"I'm smarter than that, and you should know that already. I'm at Sheila's house. I told her I needed her help again. She still has a soft spot for me, you know."

"I'll have a talk with Ajani right now. I'm sure he will come up with something."

"Let's hope so. It doesn't look like he is going to weasel out of this one, Sonia. Be very careful."

I don't know how we are going to get out of this mess. It seems as if my life is riddled with drama and more drama.

"Ajani, I have something very important to tell you. Please sit down."

"What is it now, Sonia? I'm waiting for a very important call, so please make it quick."

"Are you waiting for Charles to call you?"

"In fact, I *am* waiting for him to call. How did you know? Don't tell me *you* are psychic now."

"No, I am not psychic. Charles and Alike set you up. Charles is behind everything. He bailed Alike out of jail last night and told the authorities where we are. They will be here by midnight."

"Where did you get this foolishness from? Charles is very involved in our operations and would be a fool to double-cross me. I have as much stuff on him as he has on me."

"Well, he *has* double-crossed you. If he tells you he is going to fly in tomorrow evening, then you know my source is telling the truth. You need to talk to your father immediately so he can round up the troops. Once the authorities enter the compound and see the conditions of some of the children, he will be locked up, too."

"I'll talk to my father right away. I'm so sorry I got you involved in all of this mess. If what you are saying is true, then we truly have no place to go. I'm sure Charles told them about you and the real estate being in your name. We might have to stay in my father's world after all."

"We will recover from this, Ajani. I have faith everything will work out. I have some good news. Queen Mother's grandchildren are Ashley's daughters. I've found my nieces, and know God would not give me this blessing and then take it away."

"I didn't even know Ashley liked men, much less had children. How did you find out about them?"

"My mother finally told me, and my plan was to look for them when we left here."

"Well, let me not waste anymore time, and go talk to my father right now."

"I'm going with you, Ajani."

✳✳

"Dad, we have a problem. My business partner and best friend turned on me. The officials will be here soon to arrest me. I can't go to jail, Dad."

"You are in luck. We have several underground tunnels on this property. The tunnel leads to a deeply wooded area. We will need to leave here immediately. It will take us a few hours to get to this area. There is a bus there we can drive to my home in Detroit."

"Thank you for helping me. Excuse me, my phone is ringing and I need to take this call."

"Hi, Charles, what's up? What time will you be here tomorrow?"

"There has been a change in plans. Alike's former fiancée bailed her out last night, so I will be flying into your location tomorrow evening. I can't quite remember where you are exactly. Give me the directions again."

"Charles, there is no address for this place. I'm going to have to call you back with the exact stats. I thought I left all of the information on the plane."

"I'll look for it. In the meantime, get your things packed so we can fly out of there immediately."

"Sonia, you were right. Charles and Alike set me up. His stupid ass doesn't know the documents I have on him will put his ass in jail for a long time, though. Dad is rounding up the members, and we will be leaving in a few minutes."

"How are we going to get out of here? Where are we going? I can't believe this shit. How long have you and Charles been friends?"

"My father said this place has a lot of underground tunnels, and we are going to take the one that will lead us to the bus. We are going to Detroit. We don't have to worry about money because Pops is loaded.

King Aomar left everything to his ass.

"As for Charles and I, we have been friends for several years. We were fresh out of college when we began working as tellers at a bank. Even though we were well educated, it was difficult for us to get promoted because we were Black. Our lives changed when a customer named Alfred Koko offered us a deal we could not refuse. We had to leave England and relocate to Nigeria, and we jumped at the opportunity. My stepfather warned me about the dangers of Nigeria, but I didn't care. I wanted the money and opportunity. Mr. Koko said we would become millionaires in a year. We did not know our decision would change us for the rest of our lives.

"Alfred Koko owned a modeling and talent agency, and we were hired to manage the operations. We later found out the modeling agency was a front for the illegal trafficking of women to Europe. We were both responsible for over twenty employees who canvassed the streets looking for potential models. Our job was to seduce these women and force them into prostitution. We told our victims we had modeling gigs for them in Italy and Paris with top designers. There were so many women desiring to become models, it was easy to convince them. We never made millions as Mr. Koko claimed. He pimped us just like he pimped the women. We lived comfortably, but we were greedy young men and wanted our millions.

"Charles is a great organizer, and he can put together a plan in a matter of minutes. Gay sex in Nigeria is illegal and, if caught, can result in death. Mr. Koko was in the closet and paid extra attention to Charles. From time to time, he would give Charles a little extra money on his paycheck. Charles came up with the ultimate plan, and it was for us to take over Mr. Koko's business. Mr. Koko invited Charles to his home for dinner. We knew that Mr. Koko was an aggressive man and would try to force Charles into having sex with him. I was supposed to slip into the room and videotape the whole scenario. We were only supposed to use the tape to bribe Mr. Koko, but unfortunately, that is not what happened."

"What happened? Did Mr. Koko get a piece of Charles' ass?"

"No, but Charles did underestimate Mr. Koko's strength. Charles almost lost his virginity that night. Charles had a switchblade with him, and the minute Mr. Koko grabbed Charles' balls, he stabbed him in the chest. Since I was videotaping everything, I was not prepared for what Charles did. Charles was like a madman, stabbing Mr. Koko over and over again. It took me a long time to get him off of the man. We did not want to leave there empty handed, so we got the information we needed to run the business."

"Does Charles know you still have the videotape?"

"I told him I got rid of the evidence."

"Ajani, you should have known you could never trust Charles. I think he planned to kill Mr. Koko from the beginning. What does he have on you?"

"It was Charles' idea to make me the president of the companies we started and he would remain in the background. So, everything is in my name. But, what he doesn't know is three years ago I transferred the escort business into his name. You see, I threw him for a loop when I asked him to transfer the company to Alike's name prior to coming to South Carolina. I could tell he didn't want me to, so I suggested he use my birth name instead. I knew at that moment he was planning to set me up."

"So he should know by now the company is really in his name since he did the transfer, right?"

"That was another trap I set for him. He never did the transfer because he would have said something by now. He always thought he was smarter than me."

"How did Alike get in the picture? Was she one of the women you got into prostitution?"

"Charles met Alike at a fashion show she was modeling in, and he fell in love with her immediately. I think they would have been together if she didn't meet me. Alike is a bitter old woman, and she's still upset with me for not marrying her."

"What are we going to do now? Where is the tape?"

"I have the tape in a safe place. Everything is going to be fine. Don't worry your pretty little head."

How in the hell was I not going to be worried? I was married to a conniving son of a bitch.

Chapter 31

The tunnel was dimly lit with the candles we were holding as we marched through the dark, damp, narrow tunnel. The stench in the tunnel made me vomit, and I begged Ajani to let me rest a couple of times, but he wouldn't let me. It seemed like we had been walking for hours. Queen Mother and some of the other ladies brought food and drinks for the children, but they were not allowed to eat or drink until we got out of the tunnel. By the time we did, the skies were completely black. There was a small hut-like house where we were able to use the bathroom.

"Sonia, how are you feeling now? We have a long trip ahead of us, and I think you should eat some crackers," Queen Mother inquired.

"Thanks, Queen Mother, but I am truly not hungry. What I could use is a nice bubble bath. How are you and my nieces holding up?"

"We are fine. I told the King I am not going to go with him to Detroit, so he will drop us off at a bus station in Charleston. When I get back to New York, I'll give you a call."

"Let me give you my mother's number because I don't know where I am going to end up. How did the King take you leaving him?"

"He was not happy about it, and said that if I stayed with him, things would be different. He doesn't want to be king anymore, Sonia. He wants a normal life."

"What about the followers and his other wives?"

"The majority of the group is going to follow him to Detroit, even-though he told them they did not have to."

"Where in New York are you going? I hope you're not going back to the shelter."

"The King has a lot of money and connections. I'll be going to a condo he owns in Westchester County."

"After the money runs out, what are you planning to do? I don't want my babies to suffer, Rita. Call my mother in Georgia; she'll help you. They have a home big enough for you and the children. Think about it, Rita."

"I don't want to impose on your mother and her boyfriend. We'll be fine in New York."

"Rita, call my mother if you need help. Pride is a bitch, but it won't prevent you from starving or living on the streets. I'm sure she would welcome the opportunity to make amends."

Rita and I decided not to tell the twins I was their aunt because it would be too stressful on them under the circumstances. It was very painful for me to watch Rita and the kids exit the bus in Charleston, but I knew it was the right thing to do. I felt like I would never see them again, even though Rita told me she would be in touch. Ajani comforted me as I cried myself to sleep.

When I woke up, we were in Ohio, and the King said we didn't have much longer before we reached our final destination. Quite a few of his followers decided not to take the trip to Detroit, and were dropped off in various cities along the way. Two of Isoke's daughters decided they wanted to stay with the King, but Naveli decided to leave with a young man by the name of Jabarie who was going back to his parents. I really wanted to call my mother, but couldn't because we dumped our cell phones in the trash can at the bus station. So I stared out the window, thought about all the things that happened over the last few years, and prayed things would get better.

When we arrived at the King's house, I felt so uncomfortable. I don't know what I was expecting the house to look like, but I wasn't impressed at all. The colonial brick home had five bedrooms and three and one-half baths, and it smelled like it had water damage. The house was not big enough for all the people that decided to remain faithful to the King. Ajani assured me that we would only be there a couple of days, and then we would be going to Nebraska. I was too emotionally drained to inquire further, so I found a comfortable spot on the floor and fell asleep.

When I woke up, I noticed Ajani was gone. I panicked as I looked all over the place for him, but he was nowhere to be found.
Noticing the look on my face, the King said, "Ajani had some very important matters to take care of. He'll call you in a few days, when he has arrived at his destination."

"What? Ajani left without saying goodbye. I don't understand," I cried.

"Sonia, you will be well taken care of here. Don't worry, I don't bite."

"Why did he leave me? I can't stay here without him."

"Sonia, your husband is in a lot of trouble. It will take a long time for him to get out of this mess. He made some really poor decisions and will eventually have to face up to them. He left because he did not want you to get in trouble because of his choices."

"So he is not coming back to Detroit, is he? Be honest with me, please."

"No, he is not coming back. He is a fugitive, and you probably will never see him again. I am sure Ajani didn't share everything with you, because he didn't with me. I did my own research on him, and my son is guilty of a lot of things. If he is caught, he will have to do some serious time. You are free to stay with me in Detroit as you piece your life back together, but my advice to you is to move on, because Ajani is gone for good."

"Thanks for being honest with me. I don't think I want to live in Detroit, though…no offense to you. I appreciate all you have done for me."

"Are you prepared for the authorities to question you about Ajani and his whereabouts? They'll want to know everything."

"I don't know anything at all. Ajani is a very mysterious man, and I believe he only told me enough to get me to trust him. I married a stranger. Oh yeah, and you don't have to worry about me turning you in."

"Turn me in for what? I have not committed a crime. I am concerned about you, because you are married to him and they can consider you an accomplice."

"An accomplice to what? I did nothing wrong. After they interrogate me, they will know I was an innocent bystander caught up in some mess."

"Ajani told me to give you fifty-five thousand dollars."

"Thanks, I'm going to need it. How soon can you get me the hell out of here?"

"Would you like to leave tonight? I'm sure we can arrange a flight for you, if you don't mind flying on Delta. I don't own a private jet like your husband," the King said with a chuckle.